UNLEASHED BY THE

MOON

NEW YORK TIMES AND USA TODAY BESTSELLING AUTHOR

L.P. DOVER

ROYAL SHIFTER SERIES

L.P. Dover
Copyright © by L.P. Dover
Edited by: Briggs Consulting
Cover designed by: RBA Designs

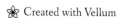 Created with Vellum

ONE

FAITH

Summer in Wyoming.

Everything about it is pure heaven to me. As I walk out the cabin's back door toward the forest, the sun shines down through the trees, leaving rays of light in sporadic places; it's breathtaking. Even if I weren't a shifter and drawn to nature, I'd still think it was otherworldly. In all reality, it is. Shifters aren't the only magical beings on earth. I've heard of fallen angels, vampires, and even demons, but the only other creature I've met was a fae prince who pretty much put my pack right in the middle of a faerie war. Thankfully, we didn't lose anyone, but it did make my life harder.

The problem is I'm an unmated twenty-six-year-old royal arctic wolf, the last female royal in my pack. That alone makes me a target, both good and bad. That's why I have Micah—my protector—to watch over me. For years, we hid away after my parents and some of the other Royal pack members, including Micah's parents, were slaughtered. For a long time, everyone thought the royal arctics were dead, but now we've reunited, at least, some of us. Micah found his two brothers, and now I have my older brother, Colin, who is still unmated and loving life, and my sister, Bailey, is mated to the Teton pack alpha, Ryker. They just had a son, which officially makes me an aunt. Maybe one day I'll get to find my mate and have children of my own. Do I see that happening? No. I've never gotten the chance to see the world. One way or another, that has to change.

Taking in a deep breath, I look up at the sliver of blue sky through the treetops. The ground is soft beneath my bare feet from the late-night rain. Everywhere I look, the grass glistens; the perfect painting. I take it all in and remember every detail to put it on a canvas later.

My thoughts are interrupted when I hear something behind me. *Footsteps.* They are very light and not meant to be heard, but I can sense them—a predator stalking its prey. I'm strong, taught to fight, even to the death if that's what it takes.

Closing my eyes, I concentrate on the wolf closing in on me. He's in human form by the smell of his skin. When we become our wolves, there's more of an earthy scent to us.

"Did you honestly think you could sneak up on me?" I call out.

Laughter erupts behind me. "Maybe. You had that daydreamy look on your face you get when you're not paying attention to your surroundings."

Slowly, I turn around and glare at my friend and protector, Micah, with his whitish-blond hair and stark blue eyes, wearing only a pair of black gym shorts. Women everywhere always tell me how envious they are that I have him all to myself. It's not what I want. What I want is for him to separate from me and find his mate. He deserves to be happy.

"That's what I wanted you to believe," I tell him. "If I appear distracted, others get careless and think I'm easy prey."

Micah shakes his head. "Yeah, but you let me get too close to you. That's a dangerous game, Faith."

"But I knew it was you," I say, wishing he'd ease up on me.

All he wants is for me to be able to defend myself, and I know I can do that. I've spent my whole life training to fight. There has to be more to life than this. Lifting my arms over my head, I stretch my muscles out. "What's on our agenda today?"

Micah squats a few times and stretches out his legs. "We have a landscaping job at the MacEntire house this morning. I figured we'd train and then head over."

Nodding, I follow his lead and work on my legs. Back when we were in hiding, we were always in the yard working together. He'd cut the grass, and I'd pay attention to the details in the gardens. A couple of months ago, we decided to start up our own business, Lyall Landscaping. Micah doesn't need the money, but I know he enjoys it. I love gardening, and so did my mother. Doing it makes me feel close to her, like she's right there with me.

We stretch in silence, but I can feel his eyes on me. "What's wrong, Faith? I can always tell when something's on your mind." He should already know because I've had this spiel with him numerous times, and every time he tells me to forget it. I look over at him, and he turns his head. "Seriously, Faith? Again, with that nonsense. How many times do I have to tell you I'm not going anywhere?"

Feeling my impatience wear thin, I jump to my feet. I don't know why I ever thought I could get him to back down. "That's the problem," I snap. "Don't you want to get away from me, to live your life without constantly worrying if I'm in danger? I want more for you. I feel like I'm keeping you from your mate. She's out there somewhere."

Micah's jaw holds firm, and he stands. "I have no doubt, Faith, but my duty is here with you. I made a vow, and I'm going to keep it." My wolf stirs inside of me, desperate for the freedom she's never been allowed to have. I'd give anything to run through the woods by myself and to travel wherever I want. I don't have the heart to sneak away in the middle of the night because I know all he'd do is search for me. That's not the kind of life I want for him. Micah blows out a sigh and places his hands on his hips. "If you want me to break my vow, I will," he states, staring at me with a twinkle in his eyes. "You know what you have to do."

Groaning, I close my eyes. We've been through this a million times. He's a royal arctic alpha, one of the strongest shifters in the world. I may be a royal too, but my strength will never be greater than his. Will I accept the challenge? Hell yeah.

I crack my neck and smile. "You're on."

His eyes glow for a second, and then he smiles. "I'm ready."

I lunge first, and he jumps out of the way, grinning smugly like he always does when I miss him. All it does is fuel my anger more. I want my freedom so bad I can't seem to think of anything else these days. Why can't he see that's what I need? He knows me better than anyone else.

Fire burns within me, and I embrace it. I use every ounce of strength I have to attack him. He dodges me left and right, but I don't back down. Sweat pours down my back, and my heart races so fast I'm afraid it's going to burst. Out of all my training, something has to give. Micah never fights the same. He does it on purpose so his opponent can never figure out his next move. It's a skill I've tried to hone, but he's had many more years of experience than me.

Sucking in a quick breath, I veer off to the left instead of the right and turn my body away from him, sweeping my left leg behind his, knocking him off his feet. He lands on his back with a loud thunk. Without hesitation, I pin him to the ground, my body aching from exhaustion.

Micah looks up at me, wide-eyed and surprised. "Not bad."

I want to celebrate my win, but I'm tired, both mentally

and physically. Micah knows it too. His smile fades, and he sighs, but I cut him off before he can speak. "You could be so much happier if you just let me go. I promise I'll be okay." My eyes burn, but I refuse to cry. "I want you to be happy."

His blue eyes stare right into mine. "I *am* happy, Faith." His muscles tense underneath my grasp, and the next thing I know, I'm on my back, sucking in a strangled breath as the wind gets knocked out of me. He straddles my waist and winks. "Your emotions made you lower your guard."

I've failed again. Growling, I prepare to push him off of me, but then the ground beneath us rumbles. Tree roots shoot up out of the grass and wrap around Micah's wrists and ankles, jerking him off of me. He hits the ground hard, and a giggle echoes from behind me. I smile as I look over my shoulder at Laila, looking angelic in her white sundress and her bright red hair in loose waves down her back.

"I think Faith won," she teases as she walks toward us.

I get to my feet, and Micah tries to fight against the roots, but they tighten around him. "She has to beat me without your magic," he calls out.

Laila is a royal arctic just like us, but she's also half-fae. That's where her magic comes from. She's mated to my good friend, Cedric, and they are expecting their first child in about five more months. Our pack is growing fast with all the newly mated females having babies, all of which will be considered royal.

Brushing the dirt off my clothes, I walk over to Laila. "What made you stop by?"

Her grin widens. "Honestly, I wanted to watch you guys train. I miss being able to spar with you both."

"And cheat by using your magic?" Micah grumbles, huffing with impatience.

Laila bursts out laughing and holds a hand on her belly. "That too." She turns to me and winks. "Another reason I'm here is to see if you could find some time to come by and look at the nursery. Cedric just finished painting the walls, but I was hoping you could add some finishing touches since you're the artist around here."

Ideas already start circulating through my head. "I would be happy to. Let me change clothes, and I'll head over before Micah and I have to be at our job."

Laila squeals. "Perfect. I'll see you there." She flicks her wrist in the air, and the tree roots immediately unwind from Micah's body. He jumps to his feet and glares at Laila, but then he shakes his head and smiles. "You know I love you," she says to him.

He waves her off. "Yeah, yeah, yeah."

She giggles and moves closer to me. "I tried."

"I know."

Turning on her heel, she makes her way back to the front of the house. I can feel Micah's eyes on me, but I keep my back to him; I dread facing him. "Shall we get back to training, or are you done?"

With a heavy sigh, I can still feel the weight on my chest. I wish he could understand how I feel. The guilt. The frustration. It hurts my heart to no end. "I'm done," I say, feeling more defeated than I ever have before.

Micah blows out a breath and moves closer. "What's changed in you, Faith? Things are different between us."

He places a hand on my shoulder, and I turn to him. He's over a hundred years old, but he doesn't look a day over twenty-five. I take his hand and hold it between mine. One day, he's going to make the perfect mate.

"I love you, Micah. You've been my only family for a very long time." I squeeze his hand and pull him closer. "Ever since we joined the Teton pack and reunited with our families, I've seen the way the others live their lives. I appreciate you keeping me safe, and I'll always and forever be grateful for your sacrifices, but when is it going to end? When are *you* going to live your life? And also, when am I going to live mine?" A tear slips down my cheek. "You have to let me go at some point."

His gaze saddens as he wipes my tear away with his thumb. "I know."

"You do?"

He nods. "I'm not an idiot, Faith. One day you'll find a mate, and you won't need me anymore."

Hearing that breaks my heart. "I will always need you, Micah. We may not share the same blood, but you're my family. All I know is that we both could use some freedom."

Deep down, I know he has to want the same thing. Micah stares right into my eyes, and I'm prepared to hear him say it's not going to happen, but that's what comes out of his mouth.

"Okay," he says, making my heart stop.

"Okay?" I reply. "Okay, what?"

He chuckles lightly and steps back. "I'll give you some freedom." Eyes wide, I start to shout for joy, but he holds up a hand. "It's only a little bit, Faith. I'm not letting you go completely."

I fling my arms around him. "Hey, at least it's a step in the right direction."

He hugs me back. "Come on. We have to get to Laila's and then head to the MacEntire's."

Squeezing him hard, I kiss his cheek and let him go. "Thank you. This means a lot to me."

He snorts. "Just stay out of trouble. Can you do that for me?"

I salute him. "You got it."

TWO

FAITH

Today has been the best day of my life so far. Everything is coming together just the way I want. Micah and I finished our job at the MacEntire house early, which left me plenty of time to take a shower and get ready for my evening out. He agreed to let me venture into town on my own with Amelie so we can shop. When you think about it, it sounds ridiculous. I'm in my mid-twenties and going out alone without my protector for the first time in my life. Then again, I deserve the freedom. There is much to celebrate tonight.

I can hear Amelie's car turn down our driveway. We both joined the Teton pack around the same time, and now we live together. As soon as her car comes into view, I rush out onto the front porch. I received an important phone call earlier and have yet to tell her.

She gets out of the car and whistles at me. "Don't you look sexy showing off those long legs of yours."

Since it's summertime, I chose a pink sundress with a sleeveless denim jacket to add to the outfit. Even though the temperatures are warm, it still gets chilly at night. Not that it matters to a shifter. Amelie walks around to the passenger's side where a box filled with school supplies sits in the front seat.

"I could say the same to you," I reply, watching her bend over to get the box with her short skirt on. Amelie looks the same age as me, but she's actually a couple of decades older. Shifters can live to be hundreds of years old. Unfortunately, the leading cause of death for our kind is other wolves. "It's a good thing you work with little kids. If you were a high school teacher, those boys would be drooling all over you."

Amelie chuckles and tucks her caramel-colored hair behind her ears before picking up her box. "It's a good thing I'm not. I don't need any of that nonsense. My students are done with school so none of them saw me in my little skirt. All I had to do was clean up my classroom and say goodbye to the other teachers." Holding the box in her arms, she uses her foot to shut the car door. "I'll probably work at Blake's ranch this summer to earn some extra income."

Grinning wide, I move out of the way so she can come up the stairs. "That sounds like fun."

Her brows furrow as she walks up. "Why are you grinning like that?"

"Oh, I don't know. I might've gotten a phone call this afternoon from a certain elementary school principal."

She gasps. "Please tell me you got the job?"

Excitement bubbles in my veins. "I did. You're looking at your school's new art teacher."

Amelie squeals and drops her box on the porch, flinging her arms around me. "Faith, I'm so happy for you. You're going to love the kids."

I hug her hard and laugh. "It's only for two days a week, but it'll give me time to help Micah with the landscaping business on the days I'm not working." With not having any teaching experience, I didn't think the school would hire me. I showed them a portfolio of my work, and Amelie made sure the principal knew I had paintings for sale in the art gallery in town.

Amelie lets me go. "You were right. We do have to celebrate tonight. Are we thinking dinner and shopping?"

She doesn't know that Micah will be staying behind. "That's exactly what I'm thinking. Go put your stuff up so we can leave. I don't want to waste any more time."

Her gaze roams toward the inside of the house. "Micah's not here. Don't we have to wait for him?"

I shake my head. "Nope. We came to an understanding this morning. It's about time I had a little bit of freedom."

Amelie's eyes narrow. "And he gave in just like that? Why do I feel like he's just pulling your tail?"

"Nice pun," I say, rolling my eyes. Then again, what if he is? I already know the story between Sebastian and my sister, Bailey. She thought she was living life independently for years, but Sebastian was there in the shadows, watching over her. It'll piss me off to no end if Micah does the same with me. I wish he could see I want this freedom for us both. Looking out at the woods, I concentrate on the surroundings, but I can't feel Micah anywhere. The thing about royals is we can hide our presence. It's one of the things which makes us lethal in attacks. If he's around, he'll definitely hear me. "He better not be trying to pull one over on me," I shout. "If he is, he'll regret it." It's all words, but it feels good to say them. Micah knows he's stronger than me. Yes, I can get in a few hits, but in the end, he always manages to best me.

Amelie shrugs. "Just saying I find it kind of odd that he would agree to this. Micah's an honorable man. If he made a vow to protect you, then it's what he's going to do."

Blowing out a heavy sigh, I nod toward the door. "Let's get ready to go. I have a strange feeling I'm going to be looking over my shoulder all night to see if I can find him."

She smiles. "I get you want your freedom, but the Lyall brothers are very handsome men. I'm shocked Micah's not your mate."

I snort. "The goddess of the moon knows better than to put him as my mate. Micah is like a brother to me." I agree with her that all the Lyall men are handsome. Micah has two older brothers, Sebastian and Zayne. They all three look alike with their whitish-blond hair and striking blue eyes. Sebastian is mated already, but Zayne is still on the market, much to his dismay. He prefers solitude to being chased for his status by women everywhere. When we get together with some of the surrounding packs, the women fawn all over Micah. I keep hoping he'll find his mate. When he does, he'll have no choice but to put me aside. In our world, mates are above all else. Unfortunately, he hasn't found her yet.

Amelie picks her box up and laughs. "Look on the bright side, when you find *your* mate, he can step aside. All the females around here will be happy when you do."

"Yeah," I grumble, "if I even find my mate. Kind of hard to do that with a bodyguard following me around. Not to mention, a royal arctic alpha."

She winks. "The betas won't come near you, but I know an alpha will. There are plenty of them around. Our pack happens to be friends with several." That's true, but it's not often we see them.

Shaking my head, I plaster on a smile. "Okay, no more talk about mates or overbearing alpha protectors. It's time we have some fun."

Amelie nods. "Deal. Let's get out of here."

She carries her box inside, and I follow her so I can grab my keys and purse. I'm ready for the night.

"MY BISON STEAK WAS ABSOLUTELY DELICIOUS," Amelie mumbles with her mouth half full.

Nodding, I finish off the last bite of my steak. "Yes, it was."

Her gaze lingers over toward the bar and then back to me. "There are two men at the bar who haven't been able to stop staring at us since we got here."

Very casually, I glance over my shoulder at them. In human years, they look to be around their mid-twenties and incredibly good-looking. Both are human and dressed in plaid button-down shirts and jeans with dark brown hair and the other a dirty blond; very cowboyish, which I've grown to love since I moved to Wyoming from Canada. Amelie got me started watching the TV show *Yellowstone,* and I'm hooked.

The guy with blond hair nods at me, and I do the same to be polite. When I turn back to Amelie, I lower my voice. She has a dark past where she was mated to another wolf, but it didn't end well. I try not to bring it up because I know it pains her.

"How many men have you slept with?" I ask her.

She takes a sip of her water. "As far as wolves, just one. Human men, six."

I envy her. I've thought about what it would be like to be intimate with a man. Don't get me wrong, I enjoy myself when I'm alone in the privacy of my home, but it's not the same. Most women at my age have at least fallen in love a couple of times. I've never been given a chance.

"Was it nice being with human men?"

Amelie smiles. "Very nice. Human men are different from our kind. They're a little more fragile, so you have to be careful. You can't be getting all hot and bothered in bed and have your claws rake down their backs. You'll rip them in two."

"Ouch. Yeah, that wouldn't be good."

She shakes her head. "Not at all. Sometimes it's exhausting, though. You can't fully be yourself with human men. Also, getting attached isn't wise because we all know it'd never work. They age, and we don't. They're only good for a short-term fling."

Sighing, I look over my shoulder at the two men again. "I'm not really interested in a fling."

"Neither am I," Amelie says, drawing my attention back to her. "I'm happy with the way my life is right now." Her gaze saddens when she meets my eyes. "But I know you haven't been able to live yours. Hopefully, you'll get the chance soon."

The waitress comes over, and we pay our bills. When we get outside, the temperature has cooled off, and it feels heavenly. I love downtown Jackson Hole. There are shops lined up and down the street with tourists everywhere. The summer is the prime time peak season for the hiking enthusiasts who want to venture into the Grand Teton National Park. It's very different from the small Canadian town Micah and I moved from. I was born in Canada, so it'll always be my home, but it changed when my parents were murdered. After that, nothing felt like home. I was torn away from my siblings just to keep us safe.

Amelie bumps me with her shoulder. "I'm thinking a walk by the art gallery to see your paintings and then to Udderly Delicious for an ice cream sundae?"

I turn to her and smile. "Sounds perfect."

The art gallery is on the next street over, and when we walk by the window, there's a woman inside buying one of my paintings. It's one of the best feelings in the world. Amelie squeezes my arm and lets out a shriek. "Would you look at that? She's buying your cottage painting."

My eyes start to burn. That cottage is the replica of the one Micah and I lived in. I can see it all as if it was just yesterday that we left it. It still belongs to Micah, and I hope he never sells it. One day, I want to go back and see it again. It's a moderately sized yellow cottage that looks as if it came out of a fairy tale. I even planted every single flower in the garden.

"It's such a beautiful place, Amelie. You would love it." I pointed at the painting. "The mountains in the background were really there. I would stare at them for hours."

Amelie clasps my arm and pulls me away from the window. "It's a good thing you have the Tetons to look at now. I have to say I love this area. It's nothing like my home in North Carolina."

I link my arm with hers. Her parents were murdered by other wolves, just like mine. She hasn't been back to North Carolina since joining the Teton pack. I never thought we'd have so much in common.

We turn the corner, and Udderly Delicious is about five shops down from where we are. There are people everywhere, laughing and smiling as they go in and out of the stores. It's interesting to watch them, knowing they're oblivious to what's really around them.

"What sundae are you going to get?" Amelie asks. "I think I want the mudslide, and I'll have them add the fudge cake."

"That sounds like heaven. I'll ..." Before I can finish my sentence, both Amelie and I freeze. Someone is near us, and it's not anyone from our pack or anyone I recognize for that matter.

Amelie's arm tightens around mine. "You've got to be kidding me. Who the hell is in our territory?"

"I don't know, but he's definitely an alpha." We both scan the crowd, and that's when I lock eyes on him. He's tall with light brown hair and bright green eyes, dressed in a pair of jeans and a snug T-shirt that hugs his well-toned body. I don't sense any danger from him, but I can feel his need. He smiles, but then his gaze averts to something behind me. I glance back quickly, and Micah is right there, glaring in the direction of the other male. "Seriously?" I growl. "What the hell are you doing here?" Am I surprised? No. When I turn my attention back to the other wolf, he's gone.

Micah comes to my side but keeps his eyes on the crowd. "Did you really think I was going to let you go out tonight alone?" I glance over at Amelie, and she shrugs, giving me that "I told you so" look.

In all honesty, I'm not mad, but the guilt I felt before magnifies tenfold. Micah will never let me go, and it's because of me why he can't live his *own* life. "Did you recognize him?" I wonder.

He shakes his head. "No, but he's definitely an alpha and not invited as far as I know."

"What are we going to do?"

Micah turns to me, his blue eyes full of concern. "I'll call the others. Right now, I think it's best I get you and Amelie out of here."

Our pack has been through so much in such a short amount of time. I dread the thought of another pack war coming to our doorstep. When alphas start encroaching on other territories, trouble usually follows.

"Will we ever be able just to live our lives in peace?" Amelie asks as Micah follows us to my car.

Even though I didn't feel any danger from the other alpha, it doesn't mean anything. "I don't know," I answer. "I really don't know."

THREE

FAITH

My pretend freedom was short-lived. I honestly thought there could be a chance Micah would let me go, but I was mistaken. He called the other men in the pack and learned that none knew of another alpha passing through. The Teton pack is an unusual one and not like any others in the world. My sister Bailey and her mate Ryker are the main alphas of the group. Ryker is the one who started it by bringing together lost wolves from all over the place. Not only do we have royal arctics, but we have gray wolves and reds. The royal arctics are natural-born alphas, so it's not common to see multiple alphas in a pack, but it works for us. All of them are respectful of each other.

After yesterday, Micah has decided to stay close to me. We trained like usual this morning and spent the rest of the day at another landscaping job. Now we're on our way back to my cabin in silence. We've barely spoken to each other since last night. Micah periodically glances over at me, and when I turn to look at him, he makes it appear as if he wasn't watching me at all.

I keep my focus on him, hoping it'll get him to speak.

After a few minutes, he sighs and meets my gaze when we stop at the light. "I'm sorry, Faith. I didn't want to deceive you. I was going to let you go alone, but then I just couldn't do it."

"It's probably a good thing. We don't know what that guy wanted, if he wanted anything at all. He could just be passing through."

Micah turns his focus back to the road and scoffs. "He's an unmated male, Faith. He couldn't take his eyes off *you*. It's pretty clear what he wants."

"What if he turns out to be my mate? You never know."

He shrugs. "True. But coming into another pack's territory uninvited isn't the way to go. It's also strange how he went unnoticed until he wanted to be seen by you. I don't like it at all. Even I didn't pick up on his trail."

I hadn't thought about the fact we couldn't sense him. Only royals can mask their presence, and he's not one; he's a gray. There are more gray wolves than any other kind in the world. It concerns me how neither one of us could detect him. Either he's stronger than we think, or he's using magic of some kind. Whatever the circumstance may be, I hope it doesn't cause a problem.

"He could seriously be passing through town."

Micah nods. "Let's hope that's the case. We've been through too much shit already."

We come upon the downtown shops, and I really want to stop at the craft store since mine and Amelie's time got cut short last night. "Do you mind stopping by Nellie's Craft store for a few minutes so I can get some paint and more canvases? I have some new ideas for the gallery."

"Sure." He turns into the parking lot. "Have you sold anymore?"

He turns to me, and I smile. "Yep. Amelie and I saw a lady purchase one last night. She bought the cottage one."

He averts his gaze. "You loved that place. I always thought you were happy there."

"I was. And one day, I want to go back. It's where all of my inspiration to paint came to me." I know I can't go up there and live, not when my family is in Wyoming, but it'd be nice to visit now and again for a vacation.

Micah parks the car, and we get out. I can tell he's on full alert by the way he scans our surroundings. It's a Saturday afternoon, and there are people everywhere, just like last night. We walk inside the store, and I go straight to the paint aisle.

"Didn't you say you needed canvases?" Micah asks.

I nod. "Yep. They are on the far wall over that way," I say, pointing in the right direction. "Five should be good."

He chuckles. "I'll get them."

While he's gone, I browse over the various oil paints. I need only a couple of colors, so I snag them up along with a Bob Ross calendar. I notice someone in my peripheral, and when I look over, it's a man who seems oddly out of place perusing over the paint selection. He doesn't seem to be interested in them at all. His hair is a light ashy brown, and he has the body of a shifter. What really makes the hair on the back of my neck stand up is I can't sense anything about him. It's like he's a blank slate. He glances over at me and smirks as if he knows something I don't. All I know is he's not human, and he's not a royal arctic to be able to conceal himself this way. Micah comes to my side, holding the canvases, and when he sees the guy, he sets the canvases down on the shelf.

He leans in close. "We're going to walk out of the store and go left around the side of the building. I promise we'll come back for your paint."

I put my paints back along with the calendar. Micah always has a plan, and I trust him. He follows me out the door, and I go left just like he said. He grabs my hand and gently pushes me against the brick building. "Stay right here."

I nod and watch him walk toward the edge of the building. When the guy from the store turns the corner, Micah grabs him around the neck and slams him against the wall. The guy doesn't even fight him; he stands there and laughs.

"Who the fuck are you, and what are you doing in Jackson?" Micah growls.

Instead of answering Micah, he looks over at me. "My name's Orin, and I'm here to see *you*."

"Why?" The word slips out before I can even stop myself.

Orin focuses back on Micah and holds up his hands. "I'm not going to hurt her if that's what you're worried about. I know you're her protector, not to mention a royal arctic alpha. I'd be stupid to take you on."

Micah pushes his arm harder into his neck. "Make one move toward her, and you're dead."

"Micah," I say, taking a step closer. "Let him go. If he tries anything stupid, I'll kill him myself."

Micah slowly lets him go, and Orin's grin widens. He runs a hand down his shirt and then rubs his neck where Micah left marks on his skin. I take another step forward. "How did you know Micah was my protector?"

Orin clears his throat and takes in a deep breath as he looks around the town. "Word has spread far and wide about you, little wolf. Everyone knows about the last royal arctic female, Faith Storm, and how the Royal pack is gaining phenomenal amounts of power."

The breath hitches in my lungs. "The Royal pack was slaughtered decades ago. I should know because my parents were among them."

Orin crosses his arms over his chest and casually leans against the wall. "Yeah, I know about all of that. The Teton pack is now considered the Royals. Word about your pack has spread all across the world." He slides a glance over to Micah before turning back to me. "You have an unmated royal protector and his royal arctic brothers, one of whom is mated to a gray. You have an older sister who mated with the Teton alpha and your unmated royal arctic brother. We all know what happens when a royal bonds with a normal wolf." His lips pull back slyly. "They share power. Your mate would become a royal."

And now it all makes sense.

"You want my power, is that it?" I snap.

Orin pushes off the wall, but he keeps his distance. "There will be more coming to find you. This is just beginning. You deserve someone strong. The men want to see if they could be your potential mate."

I can't believe my ears; it's the most ludicrous thing I've ever heard. What I do know for sure is I have to keep my mouth shut. There *are* other female royals out there; only they're still in hiding. I refuse to let them become targets.

"So basically, if there were a wolfy version of *The Bachelorette*, I would be the next contestant?"

Orin smirks. "Basically, yes. Only the show would be slightly different."

Micah grabs him by the shoulder. "I think I've heard enough. You need to get the fuck out of here."

Orin holds up his hands. "All right, I'll go. I'm not here for a fight." By the gleam in his eyes, I don't think that's true. He's a wolf and a strong one, even though he's not making a move against Micah. Still, I have no doubt Micah could rip off his head in a second. After all of the betrayals I've seen in my life, I've learned not to underestimate anyone. Orin winks at me. "I'm sure we'll be seeing each other again."

Shivers run down my spine as if his words are an unspoken promise. I'm not afraid of him or any male for that matter, but what he said about everyone knowing about me doesn't settle well. If more wolves come for me, there will be bloodshed.

Orin saunters off as if nothing amiss just happened. Jaw tense, Micah takes my arm, keeping me close as we hurry back to his car. "This isn't good," he growls, his attention focused on our surroundings. I don't sense another wolf around, but it's not like that matters. Orin and the other unknown wolf from yesterday have someone helping to conceal them.

When we get to the car, Micah opens my door, and I hop in. "What are we going to do?"

Micah glances over his shoulder and sighs. "I'm going to call the others. If what that cocksucker says is true, we're in some serious trouble."

He shuts the door and hurries around to his side to get in. The engine roars to life, and he steps on the gas. As I look in the side-view mirror, I see him ... the unknown wolf from yesterday, standing close to where we were parked. Quickly, I turn my head to see out the back window, but he's gone.

"What did you see?" Micah asks, pressing harder on the gas.

Dread settles into the pit of my stomach. I close my eyes and take a deep breath, but it doesn't help. "Orin's speaking the truth," I say, meeting his gaze. "I think the one we really should be worried about is already here."

FOUR

FAITH

"I can't believe that happened today." With her arms crossed over her chest, Amelie stares out the living room window at Micah. He's been on the phone for the past two hours, pacing the yard.

I grab a bottle of water out of the refrigerator and join her. It's late, which means it's dark outside, and anyone could be around. I scan the woods, wondering if I'll see glowing eyes staring back at me. With these wolves being able to conceal their presence, there's no telling where they are. Now I know how ordinary wolves feel about royals. I didn't realize how intimidating it feels to know someone could sneak up on you. "Tell me about it. I thought I was getting close to freedom, but I couldn't be further from it now." I open my bottle and take a sip. The whole cabin smells like the chicken and pasta Amelie and I cooked tonight, but my stomach's been too unsettled to eat.

Amelie snorts. "You got that right. You're going to have the whole pack watching after you now."

Groaning, I turn away from the window and sit on the couch. "Great. Just what I need."

Micah's footsteps pound up the front porch steps, and he comes through the door. Amelie joins me on the couch as we wait for the verdict. Micah looks at us both and sighs. "A meeting has been called with the surrounding pack alphas. They're all going to be here in two days. If these bastards want to start a war, then so be it. They'll lose."

I lean my head against the couch, turning my focus to the wood beam ceiling. "So, what happens now? Am I on house arrest?"

The room falls silent, and I have my answer. There's no sense in arguing because it's not going to get me anywhere. When I drop my head to look at Micah, I can see the turmoil on his face. "I'm sorry, Faith. With these wolves being able to conceal themselves, it puts them at an advantage. I don't want anything happening to you."

I nod in understanding. "What are we going to do?"

He glances over at Amelie and then back to me. "I think it's wise I stay here for a while. I know you don't want me up your ass, but ..."

I hold up a hand to cut him off. "Micah, it's fine. You can stay here. We've lived together pretty much my whole life." When we moved to Wyoming to join the Teton pack, he had a small cabin built close to mine. That way, I could have my own space, and he'd still be nearby.

Micah lifts his brows at Amelie. "Are you okay with me staying here?"

Amelie snorts. "I'm fine with it. I like having you around, especially when I win all your money at poker."

I snicker and the mood in the room lifts. Micah chuckles and raises his arms in the air. "What can I say? I suck at it."

"Speaking of cards," I say, getting to my feet. "I think it's time we break them out. I need something to get my mind off the shit going on in my life."

Amelie stands and heads to the kitchen. "Sounds good. I'll grab the kettle corn."

Micah comes over to me, his blue gaze full of concern. "It won't be like this forever, Faith. I promise. Just hang in there for a little while longer."

"I could say the same to you. One day, I'll be able to set you free."

He nods. "Yeah, when you find a mate. I just pray to the goddess of the moon it's not with one of the fucktards stalking you."

A chill runs down my spine. "Let's hope not."

WE SPENT a couple of hours playing card games, and Amelie beat Micah and me both every time. She doesn't even need a job with all the money she wins from us. It's now half past midnight, and I can barely keep my eyes open. Micah stayed downstairs for a while, most likely staring out the windows. He's now in the guest bedroom, but I doubt he'll get any sleep, just like I know I won't.

I change out of my clothes into a pair of pajama shorts and a T-shirt. Watching TV isn't going to help, so I lay on the bed and close my eyes. Being a wolf comes with many advantages, but those perks can also be nuisances. Take, for instance, hearing. I can listen to squirrels scurrying through the woods, the crickets chirping, and both Micah and Amelie's heartbeats. It's easy to shut off, but I'm on high alert.

When it's apparent sleep isn't going to come, I get up and pace the floor. Time seems to tick by slowly, but an hour has passed when I look at the clock. Sitting back down on the bed, I hang my head. I want to knock on Amelie's door, but I can tell she's asleep by the sound of her breathing. The same goes for Micah, which shocks me.

Lifting my head, I roll my neck and stretch out my arms. I have no choice but to try and sleep. Tossing the covers back, I slide into bed and bring the blankets over me. I close my eyes and block out the sounds all around me. It's not long before sleep closes in on me when a noise startles me awake. I hold my breath and listen.

Footsteps. That's all it is at first, but then their presence hits me like a ton of bricks to the chest. They want me to know how strong they are.

I suspect three alphas, one of whose scent I recognize from earlier. Orin. Only he's not the strongest of the three. Heart racing, I jump out of bed as quietly as I can. I expect Micah to charge out of the bedroom, but there's no movement coming from his room. His breaths are slow, just like his heartbeat. It's not the sound of a wolf on alert. The same goes for Amelie. I tiptoe out of my room to hers and open her door. She's passed out on the bed, and I rush over to her.

Grabbing her shoulders, I shake her and keep my voice low. "Amelie, wake up." She doesn't budge, and I know why. The second I touched her, I could feel the coldness all around her like she's cloaked in it. Magic. "You have got to be kidding me."

What terrifies me is Micah. I don't like the thought of any kind of magic being able to take down a royal arctic. My pulse pounds even harder now as the footsteps edge closer. I hurry over to Micah and open the guest bedroom door. He's on the floor with the sheets torn off the bed as if he grabbed them right before the magic took over. I slide across the floor and take his head in my hands.

"Micah, please, wake up. You can fight this. You're one of the strongest wolves I know." He doesn't respond, which terrifies the hell out of me. The door to the cabin opens, and I can hear three men enter. I'm not afraid to fight them, but I worry about what will happen to Micah and Amelie. I refuse to leave them defenseless.

Slowly, I set Micah's head down and get to my feet. The three men are still downstairs, casually walking around as if they own the place. None of them have tried to get me, which is odd because I'm positive they know I'm here. Before I can get to the door and step out, that's when one of them calls out to me.

"We know you're here, Faith. Might as well come down." His voice is strong, dominant. But yet, he says my name with affection just like a lover would.

Clenching my fists, I take a deep breath. I'm not going down without a fight. With my head held high, I walk out of the bedroom to the stairs. All three of the men look up at me. Orin stands off to the left of the living room while another shifter stands off to the right, his power not as strong as Orin's. They aren't the ones who concern me; the guy in the middle does. He's the one I saw in town first when I was with Amelie. Out of all three men, he's by far the most powerful. His emerald green eyes bore into mine and he smiles.

"I'm happy to finally meet you, Faith. My name's Killian."

I stalk down the stairs, one at a time. "Whoever you are, you can cut the crap. I know why you're here."

His brows lift curiously. "You do?"

I cut a glance over at Orin and then back to him. "Yeah, Oreo, over there explained it all."

The shifter to the right tries to hide his smile and fails while Orin's jaw clenches. Killian smirks and shakes his head. "I'm sure you have a million questions. If you come with us, I'll explain everything."

A growl escapes my lips, and I can feel my fangs and claws start to lengthen. I've never killed another wolf before, but I'll do it in a heartbeat. Killian notices the change and his grin widens. "We don't want to hurt you, Faith."

"You came into my home uninvited. Do you seriously expect me to believe that?"

A wolf's howl echoes from the forest outside, and all three of them go on alert, their eyes glowing. I know that howl very well; it's Cedric. Killian growls at Orin and the other guy and jerks his head toward the door. "They know we're here. Go!"

Orin runs out and the other guy follows, both shifting into their wolves as they take off into the woods. While Killian's distracted, I lunge for him, hoping to detain him long enough for my pack to arrive. He grabs me around the waist, and we tumble across the floor with him ending up above me, his body pressed into mine. Everything happened so fast it knocked the breath out of me.

Killian's gaze locks on my lips, and I'm almost sure he's going to kiss me, but he doesn't. It's a good thing because I'm prepared to rip off his lips with my teeth. I try to get out of his hold, but he's too strong. "Do you know how many men want you?"

I narrow my eyes. "I don't care who wants me. Trying to kidnap me isn't the way to my heart."

He chuckles. "That's not what I'm doing here, Faith. I was hoping you would *agree* to come with me. Don't you want to find your mate? It has to be hard with a protector following you around twenty-four-seven."

"What I want is none of your business."

"Oh, I think it is," he says, breathing me in. "I can smell your desire to be free. I can give you your freedom."

It's as if he can see into my soul. There is a desire inside of me to be free. "What's in it for you?" I ask.

He slowly slides off of me and takes my hand, helping me up. "I was hoping you could help me with that. No one is going to harm you if you come with me. On the contrary, you'll be treated just as you are ... a royal. Something to be cherished."

Another howl sounds through the night, much closer than before. Killian starts for the door and stops, his glowing green gaze on mine. "You could have everything if you come with me. Think about it. I'll be back for you."

He takes off in a blur, and I suck in a breath. In the room above me, I can hear Micah's heartbeat kick into overdrive. His steps race across the floor, and he's downstairs in a flash along with Amelie. He helps me up, and I can see the desperation in his eyes.

"Are you okay? What happened?"

With Killian being able to put a wolf down with whatever magic he has protecting him, nothing can stop him from getting what he wants. I honestly don't think I stand a chance against him.

"We need to come up with a game plan and fast."

FIVE

FAITH

It's not long before wolves surround the cabin from our pack, including my brother and sister. The second Bailey sees me, she rushes over and pulls me into her arms. She's a little older than me, but we look exactly alike with our whitish-blonde hair and blue eyes. Most arctic wolves have the same traits, just like gray wolves and reds. The reds are easy to pick out because their hair usually ranges from deep auburn to strawberry blonde.

Bailey holds me tight. "I can't believe this is happening to you."

"You went through something similar." And she did, only it was her mate's brother who tried to steal her away. Killian didn't use force or hurt me to make me go with him.

Bailey lets me go and cups my cheeks. "I'm just glad you're okay."

"Who's watching over my nephew right now?"

She smiles. "Asher's with Tyla, Sebastian, and little Brooke."

Ryker finishes talking to Micah, and they head straight

over to us. He stands protectively next to Bailey, just like a mate would. "Tell us everything."

"I will, but how did you know something was wrong?"

A car pulls down the driveway, and it's Cedric and Laila. Ryker nods at them and sighs. "Laila's the one who felt the magic and said it wasn't good. Cedric called, and we got everyone together."

With a hand protectively over her baby bump, Laila hurries over to us. "I thought the worst when I felt the magic," she sobs, flinging her arms around my neck.

"I'm okay," I assure her. "You don't need to cry."

"It's the hormones," Cedric adds. "She cries over stupid ass commercials too."

Laila lets me go and glares at him. "That's not the reason why I'm upset. I know the kind of wolves who were here. I'm surprised things didn't go worse than what they did."

Eyes wide, I stare at her. "There were three unmated alphas, but the main one was Killian. Do you know him?"

She hangs her head and sighs. "Yep." She meets my eyes. "I recognized his witch's essence. His name is Killian Vilkas and the witch is Tia Bishop. She comes from a long line of witches with powerful magic. I met her a few years ago when Killian brought her with him to visit us. When I felt her magic, I knew something bad was about to happen. It's a good thing we live close by, otherwise I wouldn't have sensed her."

"Who is this Killian Vilkas?" Cedric asks, his voice a low growl. I'd like to know the same thing.

Everyone turns to Laila, and she looks at us all. "Killian Vilkas is the alpha of the Blue River pack on the northeastern side of Canada. He owns the town of Baker's Ridge." My family is from Canada, but we always stayed on the northwestern side.

My sister looks up at Ryker. "Have you heard of him?"

Ryker shakes his head. "No."

"Which isn't shocking," Laila adds. "Killian liked to keep a low profile. With Tia by his side, he can do anything he wants. He's not the in-your-face kind of guy like my brother, which I think makes him more dangerous; a silent killer."

Colin crosses his arms over his chest. "And now he wants my sister."

Micah scoffs. "So do a thousand others from what we heard. We'll be overrun here if more wolves show up. It'll be a bloody mess."

Laila holds up a hand, her brows furrowed in concentration. "What I don't get is why Killian had two other alphas with him, especially if they're interested in Faith too. When he'd come around the Sierras, it was always because he needed something. The man is worth a *ton* of money."

"What are you thinking?" I ask her.

She shrugs. "I don't know. The last time he visited my old pack, a couple of our men left with him and never returned. Nothing was ever mentioned." That's very strange. Wolves are generally loyal to their packs.

Colin stands next to Micah. "I think we should hunt the fuckers down instead of waiting for them to come back. Laila could use her magic to help us find them." Micah agrees with a nod.

Cedric shakes his head, but Laila grabs his arm. "I'll do anything to keep Faith safe. For now, she has to stay with us until things get settled. We're the only ones who can protect her. With those of us who are fully mated, our power exceeds Tia's. She won't be able to take us out like she did Micah and Amelie, even if Micah is a royal."

I happen to glance over at Micah, and her words hit him hard by the despair on his face. It breaks my heart. For the first time in his life, he can't protect me.

"What about Amelie?" I say. "I can't leave her alone."

Amelie snorts behind me. "Those dumb ass wolves don't want *me*, Faith. I'll be fine by myself."

I glare at her over my shoulder. "Either you come with me willingly, or I'll make you."

Amelie throws her hands up in the air. "Fine. I'll go. I just don't want to be a burden."

Laila smiles sadly at her. They were good friends long before either of them knew me. "You're never a burden, Amelie. It'll be like old times having you both stay with me."

Cedric comes up behind her and squeezes her shoulders. "Maybe now you can have the girls watch your Hallmark movies with you instead of torturing me with them."

She smacks his hand. "You know you like them just as much as I do."

They banter back and forth while Micah takes my hands. "I am so sorry, Faith. I wish you knew how much it kills me I couldn't be there for you."

I squeeze his hands. "It's okay. We're going to get this figured out. I think you would've been proud of me. I told them I wasn't going down without a fight. And believe me, I was ready."

"It shouldn't be like that. They didn't hurt you, did they?"

Shaking my head, I lower my voice. "That's what's surprised me. Killian didn't hurt me at all, even when I attacked him. He did say he'll be back."

Micah's jaw clenches. "I have no doubt. Just stay close to Laila."

Staying close to Laila puts her and her baby in danger. There has to be another way. I need to figure it out and fast.

SIX

FAITH

Laila sets a steaming hot mug of coffee in front of me. "You've been quiet the past couple of days."

I breathe in the smell of the coffee. "Sorry. My mind's been all over the place."

She sits down at the kitchen table with me. Her red hair hangs in soft waves over her shoulders, and she has a pregnancy glow about her. We all know her fae magic is more potent than Killian's witch, but I refuse to put her in any harm. I haven't left the safety of her and Cedric's house since I stepped foot in it two nights ago. It doesn't feel like a prison, but it is. Wolves from our pack have been taking shifts guarding the area. So far, Killian and his men haven't gotten close. No one has seen them.

It's Monday morning, and the alphas from the surrounding packs are to arrive in town for the meeting. I want to be there. I've had two days to think about everything, and I came up with a plan. Will it work? I don't know, but I can't stay in Wyoming. No matter where I go, it's not safe for anyone. My bags are packed and ready.

Laila reaches into her pocket and pulls a rock out of her

pocket; I recognize it. Black carmine is a rare stone used for protection in the old days. Months ago, she used it to keep her hidden from the dark fae, but they already knew who she was and how to find her, so it didn't work the way she wanted.

Laila slides the rock over to me. "Take this. If you're able to get away from here, it'll keep Killian and Tia from finding you. Unfortunately, right now, they know you're here and who all of us are."

It's as if everything falls into place. I pick up the stone and close it in my palm. "Laila, this is exactly what I need."

Amelie walks into the kitchen, dressed in jeans and a T-shirt with her caramel-colored hair in a braid. "What'd I miss?" she asks, sitting down at the table.

I show her the stone. "Laila just gave me this. For the past two days, I've been thinking of a way to get Killian off my trail. With the stone, I think my idea might actually work. That is if the other alphas agree to it."

Amelie waves her hand impatiently for me to continue, but Cedric saunters into the room and leans against the kitchen counter. "I *really* want to hear this."

"First off," I say, sliding my chair back, "I want to be in the meeting this afternoon."

Laila raises her hand. "So do I."

Amelie huffs. "Well, damn, I'll be at Blake's ranch working. I miss everything."

Getting to my feet, I walk over to Cedric. Out of all the men in the pack, *he* is the one I know will agree with me. "Hear me out," I say to him. "This could seriously work if the other alphas are on board."

His brows furrow. "What does this have to do with them?"

Laila and Amelie stare curiously at me. My plan is bold and maybe a little scandalous in the scheme of things, especially since I do have ulterior motives. If Killian is here to steal me away and mate me off to either himself or someone else, I need to beat him to the punch. I already know my mate is not within the Teton pack. It's up to me to find my mate, on my own time. The only way to do that is to get away.

Cedric notices the black carmine in my hand and then looks into my eyes. "You want to leave, don't you?"

I nod. "I think it'll work. You and Ryker are close friends with so many of the surrounding packs. If their alphas agree to take me in, I can travel around and make it hard for Killian to find me. All I have to do is slip out undetected. He'll never believe you guys would let me go."

I look over at Laila and Amelie, and they both smile. "Not a bad idea, Faith," Laila agrees. "And who knows, you might find what you're looking for."

Cedric lets out a long sigh. "I know what this is about. This is your way of getting that freedom Micah won't let you have."

"He has to let me go, Cedric. This plan doesn't involve him; it's about *me*. I need to find my own fate, not have someone force it on me."

Understanding flashes in those gray eyes of his. If the alphas agree, Micah will *not* be going with me. "Okay," Cedric murmurs. "I get it. I think it's a great idea, and I have no doubt the other alphas will agree to it." He glances over at Laila and then back to me. "They might be a little too thrilled with the thought of having a royal, unmated female under their roof. The good thing is I know they're respectable men."

Amelie snorts. "If they aren't, Faith can put them in their place."

Cedric bursts out laughing. "I know that." His phone beeps, and he slides it out of his pocket to read the text. He types out a reply and slips it back into his pocket. "That was Tate Grayson. He's stuck away on business and won't be able to make it. He said whatever we all decide, he's good with it." Tate is alpha of the Great Plains pack, and I enjoyed talking to him when I met him at Laila's welcome to the pack party. He's handsome and a hard worker. Out of all the wolves at that party, he and Chase Maheegan, the Timberwolf pack alpha, were my favorites. Cedric walks over to Laila and rubs her shoulders. "The only issue now is Micah."

Laila shakes her head. "I don't think he'll be a problem, not when he hears what I have to say."

Cedric kisses the top of her head. "This is why I love you."

There was a time when Laila would train with Micah and me. I've seen her use her magic to open a hole in the ground and toss him in it. She's even killed people by suffocating them by closing them into the earth. If all else fails, she could trap him while I left, but that's the last thing I want to do to him. I want him to let me go willingly.

WHEN WE GET to Ryker's, all of the alphas are there. I don't know who all is inside, but I can feel their power and all the wolves around us, protecting the perimeter. My brother, Micah, and my sister, with little Asher are the only ones on the front porch. I get out of Cedric's truck and rush over to kiss my nephew on the cheek. He has the signature look of an arctic with his blond hair and clear blue eyes. He smiles, and it warms my heart. "You are just the cutest thing." I wink at my sister. "He's going to be a heartbreaker."

Bailey snorts. "Yes, I know." She gives me a side hug and sighs. "I wanted to come out and say hey to you before the meeting. It's time for Asher's afternoon feeding and a nap."

I nod. "I'll say goodbye to you before I leave." She smiles and carries Asher inside.

Colin pulls me in for a hug. "How are you holding up?"

"I'm fine. Just ready to figure this craziness out."

He lets me go, and Micah takes his place. I hug him hard and silently pray he doesn't get angry once he hears the plan.

Laila and Cedric come up behind us, and we all walk inside. Ryker and Sebastian are in the living room with three of our ally pack alphas. Ian Randale is a little older than me and the Northwestern pack leader with light brown hair and green eyes. He became alpha at fifteen years old through combat. He's extremely strong and not afraid of anything. Next to him is Colton Redding, the alpha of the Red Wolf pack. Anyone can see he's a red with his auburn hair and gray eyes. Lastly, is Chase Maheegan, the Timberwolf pack leader, with his ash-colored hair, bright blue eyes, and a friendly smile. The only person we're missing is Tate.

Chase's smile widens when he sees me, and I wave at him. "It's good to see you again. Did you ever hike up Mt. Whitney?"

He chuckles. "I did. You'll have to try it one day."

At Laila's party, we talked about his family's vineyards, but mainly, he told me about all the hiking there is where he lives. I loved listening to him tell me about all of the national parks and how beautiful they are. "I will definitely have to do that," I reply. I move to one side of the room where Colin stands on my right and Micah on my left. Laila winks at me and gives Chase a quick side glance. I know what she's thinking, but I haven't had any inclination that he's my mate.

Ryker moves to the middle with Cedric and glances around at everyone before speaking. "First of all, thank you for coming. I talked to all of you on the phone, so you know what's going on. Laila knows who these wolves are and what they're capable of. We've seen it firsthand. We know they'll be back for Faith. Right now, they can't get to her because of Laila's magic." He turns to Laila and nods. "Do you mind telling everyone what you know?"

She nods and he moves out of the way so she can stand by Cedric. "The Blue River pack is who we're dealing with right now. Their alpha is Killian Vilkas, and he's worth a lot of money. I don't know what he does to get it, but I know it can't be legal. He has a witch named Tia working for him; her family has been indebted to the Vilkas' for decades. She's strong, and we've seen what she can do. Not even a royal can withstand her magic, except for myself. That's because my power comes from the fae."

Ian crosses his arms over his chest, looking dangerous with how serious his expression is. I haven't spent any time with him, but I've noticed he's really intense. "How are we supposed to fight against her magic?" he asks.

Cedric steps forward. "We're hoping you won't have to. Faith came up with an idea that we think will work."

Out of the corner of my eye, I see Micah and Colin looking over at me. Only Ryker, Cedric, and Sebastian know about my plan. I wanted Sebastian to know so he could help convince Micah it's a good idea. As luck would have it, he agrees it is.

Micah leans in close. "What kind of idea did you come up with?"

Colin elbows me in the side. "I'd like to know the same thing."

Cedric glances at him over his shoulder and then looks at me. I nod for him to continue. "Just don't be mad at me," I whisper to both Micah and Colin. Cedric turns his attention back to Ian, Colton, and Chase. My heart thumps so hard it must be going ninety miles an hour.

"Laila gave Faith her black carmine stone. Its magic will help keep her hidden. If we can get her away from here unnoticed, it'll keep her safe from Vilkas and his men. Right now, they know she's still with us. We want to keep it that way so they'll come at us again, and we can finish it." I'm not too fond of the latter part of the plan, but I was outnumbered. The reason I wanted to leave was to keep them safe, not to put them in danger.

"I can get her out," Micah states.

Sebastian stands next to him and meets my gaze; they look so much alike. The room falls silent, and I know it's my turn to explain. "*You* won't be going with me, Micah."

His eyes blaze. "What do you mean I won't be going with you. You're sure as hell not going alone." Sebastian places a hand on his shoulder.

I shake my head. "Of course, I'm not."

Cedric clears his throat. "We were hoping to get help from the outside. That's where the other packs come in."

Ian, Colton, and Chase all look at each other, and Chase is the one who speaks up. "How can we help?"

Ryker glances at Micah and then at them. "Instead of keeping Faith in one place, she thought it would be best to stay with each of your packs for a while. Like one week with you," he says to Chase, "and then the next with the Northwestern pack," he says to Ian, "and so forth." All three alphas agree with a nod.

"Seriously?" Micah cuts in. His anger fills the room, making it hard to breathe.

Sebastian squeezes his shoulder. "You can't go with her, brother. Vilkas and his men know you are Faith's protector. Wherever you are, they'll expect her to be close. For this plan to work, you have to stay behind." Micah's jaw clenches and he looks at me once before turning on his heel and storming out the door. Sebastian gives me a sad smile. "He'll be okay. It wasn't easy for me when I had to give up your sister."

"I know," I murmur. The bond between a female and her protector is special. It was hard for Sebastian to step aside when Ryker laid claim to Bailey. Then again, it could just be because he and Micah are stubborn and overprotective.

"Faith can stay with me first," Chase suggests. We all look at him, and he smiles at me. "If that's okay with you." Ian's eyes narrow as if he's annoyed, and it doesn't go unnoticed, especially by Laila who tries to hide her smile.

I'm kind of glad Chase spoke up first. If Tate were in town, I would've wanted to go with either him or Chase. "Sounds great. We can leave tonight. I look forward to going on all those hikes we talked about."

Cedric pats him on the back. "Thanks, Maheegan. And thank you," he says to the others. "We'll be in touch with you next week."

I walk up to Ian and Colton. "I want to thank you both as well. I know you didn't have to agree to any of this."

With his smoldering gaze on mine, Ian's lips pull back slightly. "It's no problem. I look forward to the time with you."

"Same," Colton agrees. I say my goodbyes to them and head for the door. Micah is nowhere in sight, but I can sense him out in the woods with Sebastian. When I get out there, his back is to me.

Sebastian comes toward me and smiles. "He'll be okay. Don't worry about him."

It's easier said than done. I'm always going to worry about Micah. He walks off, leaving me alone with my protector. A couple of minutes pass by before he speaks. "I'm sorry I got angry. It's not easy putting your safety in someone else's hands."

"I know," I murmur. "You've always wanted what's best for me."

He finally turns around. "I could feel their need, Faith. That plan of yours is just what they want." His gaze narrows. "And I think it's something you want as well."

"It is," I confess. "You know I want to see the world. I love our pack and having our families close by, but I don't feel like this is my place. Having Killian and his men here just made it even more apparent." I reach for his hands. "I need to find where I belong. Something in my heart is telling me to venture out."

Micah looks away. "Then go. If staying here keeps Killian

from finding you then I'll do it. I just hope you find what you're looking for." He smiles at me, and I hug him.

"I hope so too. I'm going to miss you."

His grip tightens around my waist. "I'll miss you too." He lets me go, and we walk back to Ryker's house where everyone is gathered outside. "Make sure you keep the stone with you at all times. It should shield you and Maheegan both since you'll be in close quarters in the car."

"I will."

Ian and Colton leave, but Chase waits for me by his car. I walk over to him, and he opens the passenger side door for me but nods toward everyone watching us. "I'm sure they're all wanting to say goodbye to you."

I make my rounds, stopping at my sister and Ryker first. She hugs me hard and tells me I better text her every single day. Amelie says the same, and so does Colin. Cedric and Laila are next, and I hug them both.

"Keep us updated," Cedric says. "Your bags are already in the car, and I called Tate a few minutes ago. He's ready for whenever you want to stay with his pack."

"Great. I'd like that to be my next stop."

He nods. "I'll let him know. Depending on what happens here, we'll figure out how to get you to him."

Laila places a hand on my shoulder and turns me toward her, her expression serious as she meets my gaze. "Don't lose the stone. This plan of yours will work if you keep it close."

Reaching into my pocket, I feel its smoothness against my fingers. "I will."

She leans in close. "I don't know why but I have a good feeling about this. Stay safe and have fun. You have four alphas who are chomping at the bit to get you all to themselves."

Cedric chuckles. "I'm glad Chase spoke up first. You two will get along great."

I have no doubt. I look behind me, and Micah is standing at the car with Chase. They shake hands, and then he focuses on me, his forehead creased with worry lines. Chase walks around to the driver's side to give us space.

"Take care of yourself," I say to him.

Micah snorts. "You do the same. Make sure to call if you need me. I'll be right there."

"Always." I hug him one last time and get in the car.

Chase starts up the ignition, and I wave at everyone as he pulls out of the driveway. "You're going to love northern California. I'll take you to all of my favorite spots."

The thought excites me, and I smile. "I can't wait."

When we get to the main highway, he presses on the gas, separating me from my pack. The feeling is strange, but it also feels right. "So, tell me," he begins and then stops.

Tilting my head, I stare at him curiously. "Tell you what?"

The interior car lights make his eyes look like they're glowing. "Are you in love with your protector?"

My heart swells with love for Micah, but it's nothing sexual. "No," I answer in all honesty. "He's my family, and I love him. He will always hold a special place in my heart. I want him to find his mate and be happy. He can't do that following me around."

Chase nods. "I know it had to be hard for him to let you go. Hopefully, Vilkas and his men will be put down soon. I haven't felt the rage yet with being unmated, but I know how it feels to want to find your mate. I've seen how far some will go; it's not pretty."

With a heavy sigh, I lean my head against the seat. "That's what I'm afraid of." How far will Killian go to find me? Something tells me pretty damn far.

SEVEN

FAITH

ONE WEEK LATER

Being with Chase's pack for the past seven days has been truly epic. We spent most of the days exploring the national parks around his home, walking around his vineyards, and at night we'd sit by the fire pit on his back deck, drink wine and talk. No one from my pack has seen or heard from Killian since I left. Even Laila hasn't been able to track him down with her magic, which means he's no longer in the area.

The smell of pancakes wafts in the air, and I breathe it in. Chase and I came up with a plan to alternate cooking days. Today is his day to cook all the meals. I don't see how he isn't mated yet. The wolves in his pack love him, and they're loyal. The man is handsome, smart, and very attentive. He has a successful vineyard that's well-known across the country. What I love is his house. It's a Tuscan-style villa with stone walls, intricate wrought iron accessories all throughout, and stone paths that lead to the vineyards.

I look around the guest bedroom and smile. It has an earthy feel to it with its soft yellow walls and wooden beams. The windows have long, sheer curtains over them to allow the natural light to filter in. It's perfect because I have a fantastic view of the vineyards from my room. In a way, I don't want to leave, but I know I must.

My bags are packed except for the clothes I plan on wearing tomorrow. In the morning, Chase is flying with me to Tate Grayson's house in Montana. I'll be spending the next week with the Great Plains pack.

Stomach growling, I walk out of my room just as my phone beeps with an incoming text.

Micah: You doing okay?

He texts me every morning, asking the same question. Bailey does the same along with Amelie and Laila. It feels good to know I have them. I didn't realize how much I was going to miss them by being gone.

I type back a response.

Me: I'm doing great. It's so beautiful here. Chase has been an exquisite host. In a way, he reminds me of you.

Micah: Ha! He can't compete with me.

Giggling, I text him back as I walk down the stairs to the kitchen.

Me: I'll be sure to tell him that. 😊

Micah: Go for it. Just stay safe out there. Vilkas and his men are still incognito. We don't know where they are.

Me: Got it. I'm prepared to rip off some balls if I have to.

Micah: That's my girl.

When I get into the kitchen, Chase looks down at my phone and shakes his head with a smile on his face. There are two plates at the table, and both are piled high with pancakes. "You have the funniest laugh."

"Thanks," I say, taking a seat. "Micah was telling me how no one has seen Killian and his men, and I said I know how to rip off balls if they come this way."

Chase starts to sit and freezes. "Ouch. Remind me not to get on your bad side." We both laugh, and he takes his seat.

There's a bowl of warm syrup off to the side, and I use it to pour over my pancakes. "Micah taught me well." But then, that night with Killian replays over in my head. He was too strong for me to overpower him. "Unfortunately, my training couldn't help me with Killian. I have no doubt I could've hurt the others, but him ..."

Chase's eyes blaze like fire. "You're strong, Faith. Don't you ever doubt that. You were there and prepared to fight. That right there shows you have guts."

I look over at him. "Thanks, Chase. I've really enjoyed being here with you."

He tries to hide his need from me, but I feel it every time. I know he wanted something to happen between us, but the bond isn't there. Everyone says I'll know it when it happens.

"I've enjoyed my time with you as well," he replies. "Now I truly know how hard it was for Micah to send you off. I'm going to miss having you here."

"We still have one more day. Do you think we could spend it walking around the vineyards? It's so peaceful out there."

Chase smiles. "Sounds like a plan to me. And tomorrow afternoon, I have a private jet taking you to Montana. Your brother is meeting us at the airfield. Just know you can always come back here anytime you want."

"I appreciate that. My family and I are lucky to have you as an ally. It's a rarity to find true friends among other packs."

He nods. "You're right. I've been in my fair share of fights. There's a lot of deception and disloyalty out there. You never know who's going to turn on you."

And that is the stone-cold truth. My parents learned that

the hard way, and I've seen it firsthand numerous times. I hate how you never know who those people are until it's too late.

EIGHT

FAITH

The plane ride with Colin went by quickly since we talked the entire time. I haven't spent much time alone with him since I joined the Teton pack, so it was nice being able to get to know each other better. We spent way too many years separated after our parents were murdered. We've changed so much since we were children.

We land in Montana, and there's a black rental car waiting for us at the private airfield. Colin gets in on the driver's side, and we head on our way. The closer we get to Tate's house, the more it reminds me of my cabin in Wyoming being secluded in the woods. Chase lives out in the open with vast fields of grapevines. It's not easy for him to run out his back door and shift into a wolf without the chance of being seen.

"Several of the women in Chase's pack asked about you," I say, looking over at Colin.

His lips pull back in a smirk. "Oh yeah?"

I giggle. "Yep. You should probably get out and visit some of the other packs as well."

He shakes his head. "It's not that easy for us males, sis.

Men don't like it when others encroach on their territory, regardless if they're friends or not."

I shrug. "That's the problem. If we aren't finding our mates within our pack, then things need to change."

Colin chuckles. "I agree. It's just some males get a little tense with a royal arctic around."

I roll my eyes. "Yeah, yeah, yeah. Keep telling yourself that, Colin. Killian and the other alphas weren't nervous in the least being around Micah."

His jaw clenches. "That's because they have a witch helping them out. In a fair fight, they wouldn't last two minutes."

That may be the case with Orin and the other wolf, but not Killian. He has a strong wolf presence about him. That could be coming from Tia and her magic, but I don't know for sure. Laila would be able to tell, but I'm hoping she doesn't get anywhere near Killian and his men.

We turn down a long, paved road, surrounded by trees. It winds around the mountain and when we get to the top, Tate's cabin is there with a giant workshop in the back with a sign that says Grayson's Construction.

"What all does Tate do? I never asked him before."

Colin parks the car in front of the cabin. "He's a man of many talents. I'm an architect, and I design houses, but Grayson is the one who builds them. He also buys old houses and fixes them up. His company has been passed down from son to son." I look over at him and can see the sadness in his eyes. He never got the chance to have something special like that with our father.

We get out of the car, and Tate's sister, Kami, opens the cabin door. Her light brown hair is longer now, and she still has gorgeous gray eyes that I've been envious of ever since I met her many months ago. Out of all the women I've met from other packs, Kami and I clicked instantly. She waves and beckons me up onto the porch.

"You're early. I'm almost done getting your room ready."

While Colin grabs my bags out of the car, I rush up the stairs and hug her. "We should've gotten here earlier so I could help you."

She scoffs. "Please. I'm happy to do it. I've been excited to have you here. How did it go with Chase?"

I let her go and looked into those silvery-gray eyes of hers. "It went great. I enjoyed being able to see California. As you know, I haven't gotten out much in my twenty-six years of living."

"I know how that goes." She nods toward the door. "Come on, let's go inside. I made dinner for you and my brother." Then she winks. "Figured I'd do something to make you feel welcome. Plus, my cooking's rather impeccable if I say so myself. I haven't heard any complaints yet."

"Sounds perfect to me." Colin comes up behind me, and I turn to face him, draping an arm over her shoulders. "You remember my brother, Colin, right?"

Kami snorts, and I can sense a bit of sarcasm in her tone. "I do. We met at Laila's party."

Colin's lips tilt up. "If I remember correctly, I had to save you, didn't I?"

Kami waves him off. "Please. I could handle myself. It was just a human. Also, I'm not a damsel in distress."

Mouth gaping, I stare at them both. I'm starting to think Kami doesn't like my brother much. Then again, he can be a little arrogant at times. "How did I miss this?"

Colin laughs, but Kami purses her lips. "It was nothing. I was in the parking lot, and a guy stumbles by, clearly drunk I might add, and starts hitting on me. Colin comes out and scares him to the point he pisses himself."

Colin shrugs. "The dumb ass deserved it. He was about to whip out his cock, and nobody wanted to see that shit. He needs to be more respectful of women."

"Wow," I gasp. "I had no clue that happened."

Kami glares at Colin. "I had it all under control."

"You did," Colin agrees, his voice flirty like he does with all the women, "but it felt good to put him in his place."

I pat his arm. "I bet it did."

Kami waves toward the door. "Well, let's get inside so I can show you around. Tate's still in the shower, but he'll be out soon." She glances back at my brother. "Are you staying for dinner, Colin?" It's obvious she doesn't want him to, and by the smirk on his face, I know he wants to say yes just to piss her off.

We follow her upstairs and down the hall to the second door on the right. When she opens it, I walk in first, loving the homey ambiance. It's rustic-styled with a queen-sized bed, a reading nook by the window, and a fireplace on the opposite side of the room. There's even a large window overlooking the lake with the Rocky Mountains in the distance, the perfect landscape for a painting.

Colin sets my bags down on the bed. "I'd love to, but I need to get back home. I'm meeting with a client first thing in the morning."

Kami tries not to appear overjoyed and fails. "Maybe next time then." She takes my arm and leads me out of the room. The front door opens, and a guy walks in. I know I've met him before, but I can't remember his name. He's tall with medium brown hair, gray eyes, and a small scar above his right eyebrow.

Colin goes straight to him and shakes his hand. "Hey, man. How ya been?"

Kami leans in close. "That's Anson, my brother's second-in-command."

I nod. "Got it. I couldn't remember," I whisper.

She giggles. "Don't let him know that."

Anson looks at me and smiles. "I didn't think you were getting here until tonight. I came by to show Tate my new motorcycle."

Colin nudges him toward the door. "I want to see it. Been thinking of getting one myself."

"Oh yeah, that's just what you need," I tease.

Anson and Colin head outside, and we're about to follow them when I hear Tate's footsteps above us. I look up at the top of the stairs, and there he is, dressed in a pair of jeans and a plain white T-shirt with his hair still slightly wet from the shower. His hypnotic blue eyes lock on mine, and he smiles. It's been a few months since I've seen him, and I can't help but notice how hot and rugged he is, especially with the stubble on his cheeks. Out of nowhere, my heart races out of control, and I fight the urge to rub my chest.

"You're here," he says as he comes down the stairs.

"I am."

Kami clears her throat and bumps into me. "Now that Faith's here and settled, I'm going to go. Your dinner is ready in the oven."

"You're not staying?" I say, jerking my attention to her.

Her eyes twinkle, and she shakes her head. "There's somewhere I need to be. You two enjoy." She winks at me and waves as she leaves.

Tate chuckles. "Is Colin staying for dinner?"

I take a deep breath, hoping it'll slow my heart. If I can hear it pounding in my ears, then I know Tate can. When I look at him over my shoulder, I shrug. "I don't think so. He needs to get back to Wyoming."

Tate's grin widens. "Guess it's just you and me tonight."

"I guess so." Why am I so nervous? I've been around him

before and never had any issues. And now I'm going to be alone with him for a week. It's a good thing he can't read my mind because even I'm blushing with the thoughts running through my head.

NINE

Faith is even more beautiful than before. The second I saw her by the door, I had to reel myself in. I tried not to smile at the sound of her erratic heart, but I couldn't help myself. I already know nothing will happen between us, but it's nice to know I can get that kind of reaction out of her.

"What did you think of Kami's famous chicken parmesan?"

Faith savors the last bite on her plate. "It's absolutely amazing. I'm a good cook, but I think she has me beat on this one."

"Yeah, I heard about your cooking. Chase made it a point to tell me all about it." Chase is a good friend, but I know where he was going with all of his comments. He was hoping Faith would turn out to be his mate, but it didn't happen. I feel guilty for being happy about that.

Faith grabs her glass of wine and sits back in her chair. "What all did he tell you?"

I smirk. "Everything. Chase even sent me a case of your

favorite wine from his vineyard," I say, glancing down at her glass.

She looks at her wine and chuckles. "I thought it tasted familiar. It's literally the best wine I've ever tasted. I'll have to get him to ship me a case when I go back to Wyoming."

"What are you going to do if your pack can't find Vilkas?"

Smile fading, she sets her glass on the table. "I don't know. That night Killian came for me, he had a chance to hurt Micah and Amelie, but he didn't. He didn't even hurt me when I attacked him." She looks over at me and sighs. "I'm just afraid it won't be like that the next time. Micah will risk his life for me, and I refuse to let him. If all else fails, I'll travel the world on my own. I'm not a damsel in distress that needs saving."

"No, you're not," I say in all seriousness. "But I know Micah wants to keep you safe, just like I do. The only people in my pack who know you're here are my parents, Kami, and Anson. If you don't mind, I'd like to keep it that way for now."

She nods. "That's fine. Your home, your rules. I'm the outsider here."

"You're not an outsider, Faith. You're a friend of the pack. For the next week, my home is your home."

Her lips pull back into a sexy smile. "Thanks, Tate. Does that mean I have control of the kitchen?"

I burst out laughing. "Hey, if you want to cook that's fine. Just make sure you have enough for me too."

She shrugs. "I'll think about it." Then she winks. "Just kidding. I don't want to be a burden, so I'll help out around here as much as I can." She stands and reaches for my plate, but I pick it up and hers before she can get to them.

I take our dishes into the kitchen, and she follows me. "I know how to clean dishes."

"I have no doubt," she says, laughing. "Your kitchen is spotless."

After rinsing off the plates, I place them in the dishwasher.

"My mom taught me well." She wraps up the dish with the leftover food and sets it in the refrigerator. "What all do you want to do while you're here?" I ask.

She leans against the counter. "Don't you have to work?"

I shake my head. "I'm in the middle of a project, but I can finish it up after next week?"

"Don't do that," she says, stepping toward me. "You don't have to stop work because of me. Maybe I can help you. Colin told me you work on houses."

Grayson's Construction has been in my family for years. My father passed it down to me the day he stepped away from being alpha. I inherited both the business and the pack. "I do. I'm currently working on a renovation for a young couple in town. Anson and I are replacing all the flooring and windows and doing all the painting."

Her eyes light up. "It just so happens I'm an excellent painter. Mainly on canvas, but I'm sure I can help you paint the rooms."

When I met Faith all those months ago, I thought she'd be entitled because she's a royal. On the contrary, she's the most down-to-earth and genuine woman I know besides my mother and sister. I used to be envious of Cedric for being friends with her. There are plenty of women in my pack, but none have caught my eye the way Faith has. Chase made her time with him memorable, and I want to do the same. The last thing I want is her working the entire week she's with me.

"I'll finish it up next week," I say to her. "You've never been to Montana, so let me show you around. I want you to enjoy your time here."

She crosses her arms over her chest. "You think I'll be a shitty painter, don't you? That's why you don't want me to help."

I hold my hands up. "No, that's not it." I'm not about to tell her the reason is I want to spend time with her. By the determined look on her face, I have a feeling I'm going to lose this argument. "Fine," I give in. "You can come with me to work. I just figured it'd be the last thing you'd want to do."

She steps forward and places a hand on my arm, her blue eyes boring into mine. Her heart speeds up again, and so does mine. I love the way her skin feels against me. "You're helping me, so I'm going to help you. It's what I *want* to do."

"Okay. We'll get started bright and early."

"Great." Her hand slides away, and she takes a step back. "I think I'm going to turn in for the night. It's been a long day."

I nod. "See you in the morning."

She leaves the kitchen and starts for the stairs. "Good night."

"Same to you," I shout. Ever since I met Faith, she's taken over my dreams. Does it mean anything? No. All it does is remind me that she's something I'll never have.

TEN

FAITH

I thought it would take me a while to fall asleep last night, but I passed out the second my head hit the pillow. I woke up with the sun on my face and the sound of birds chirping outside my window. The view of the lake from the window is breathtaking.

I don't know what time Tate wants to leave, so I throw my hair up into a ponytail and dig through my clothes to find a T-shirt and shorts I don't mind getting ruined with paint. Before I can head downstairs, my phone rings and Laila's name pops up on the screen.

"Hey," I answer.

"Good. You're awake." There's concern in her voice.

I sit down on the bed. "What's wrong?"

She sighs. "Well, I guess it's all in how you look at it. Cedric and I went to the donut shop this morning because you know the baby wanted a glazed cream-filled one ..."

I can't help but laugh. "Yeah, okay. You expect me to believe it's all the baby."

"Oh, whatever. It's my story, and I'm sticking to it. Anyway, we were out and about, and I felt Tia's magic. Since I know what Killian looks like, I was able to spot him. He's still here, which means he's definitely not near you."

You would think it'd give me relief to know he's not on my trail, but he's still too close to my pack. "Did you tell the others?"

"Cedric's on the phone with Ryker now. I wouldn't let him confront Killian alone, even though I know he wanted to. I don't know what they'll do. This is the first time I've felt Tia's magic since you left."

"Do me a favor and stay safe. I worry about you guys."

She snorts. "We'll be fine."

I have no doubt. "Keep me updated on what's going on, okay?"

"Will do. How's it going with Tate?"

I can hear him rummaging around in the kitchen. The smell of fresh-brewed coffee sneaks its way up to my room. "Good," I whisper, breathing in the scent. "I'm a little embarrassed to face him this morning."

She giggles. "Why? What'd you do?"

I rub a hand over my chest. "I don't know what came over me, but my heart started racing the second I saw him. I have no doubt he heard it. That didn't happen when I met him at your party."

"Interesting. Did you feel anything like that with Chase?"

"No. Tate's the only one."

"Well, it could be because he's an incredibly attractive man. Don't you dare tell Cedric I said that."

"I won't," I laugh. "And yes, Tate's ridiculously hot, but so is Chase."

"Who knows, Faith. He could be the *one*. Do you have any other types of feelings? Have you touched him?"

I made a point to touch him last night, wondering if I'd feel something. "Yes," I answer. "Nothing happened."

"Bummer. You're probably just attracted to him. You'll know when your mate is close."

So I've been told. "Thanks for calling Laila. I'll let Tate know that Killian is still in Wyoming."

"I'll call you if anything changes."

We say our goodbyes, and I head downstairs to the kitchen. Tate is standing by the kitchen counter with the newspaper spread open. There's an extra cup of coffee off to the side, along with a plate of blueberry muffins. He looks up at me and smiles a little unsurely. "Morning. I didn't know if you drank coffee, but I poured you some. Also, Kami stopped by and dropped off the muffins. She wanted to make sure you had breakfast. I was fully prepared to present you with a bowl of cereal."

Laughing, I grab one of the muffins. "Thanks. I'll take both. And a bowl of cereal would've been completely fine with me. Frosted flakes are my favorite."

Tate winks. "Mine too. I have two boxes in the pantry."

"Perfect. We can eat cereal tomorrow." I take a bite of the muffin, replaying all of the things Laila just told me on the phone.

Tate's brows furrow. "Everything okay?"

I pick up my coffee and blow off the steam. "For the moment, yes. Laila called and said she and Cedric spotted Killian this morning. The good thing is that he's nowhere near here. The bad is that he's still lurking around my town."

Tate blows out a sigh. "He must really want you."

"He didn't say he wanted me for himself."

He looks at me as if I've lost my mind. "It doesn't have to be said, Faith. He's an unmated male, and he made a move on your pack. That right there is all you need to know."

"What about the others? Why would two other unmated alphas help Killian take me?"

His jaw clenches as he brings his cup of coffee to his lips. "I don't think you want to hear my answer to that."

I'm starting to think I don't. I've had my own theories, and none of them are good. Tate's thoughts are most likely in line with my own. I can't imagine all three of them are willing to pass me around, but nothing in my world surprises me anymore.

To change the subject, I glance over to the microwave clock. "What time do we need to leave?"

He finishes his coffee and places the cup in the sink. "Whenever you're ready, we'll go. I'll be outside loading things into the truck."

I take a bite of the muffin and nod. Tate smiles and walks out of the room. While he's gone, I finish the muffin and head toward the door, but stop when I notice the pictures on his fireplace mantle. I glance out the window to make sure Tate can't see me looking at them. The first picture I notice is one of him and what I assume is his dad. They look exactly alike. Tate is in a green cap and gown, holding his high school diploma. The next picture is Tate with Kami at her high school graduation, wearing the same school colors. I move on to the last image of Tate, Kami, and their parents, all posing for the picture with smiles on their faces. My eyes burn, and I look away. I didn't realize Tate had come inside until I can feel him behind me.

"I'm sorry," I say. "I got a little sidetracked looking at your photos." I glance at him over my shoulder, and his gaze saddens.

"It's okay. I know what happened to you and your family. I can't imagine having all of that taken away at such a young age."

I turn back to his photos. "It wasn't easy. I didn't get to graduate or have happy family photos. All I had was Micah and my memories. There are so many out there who think being a royal is the best thing ever. I wish they knew how screwed up it actually is. All my family has seen is war. We have to look over our shoulders and wonder what's coming at us next. Even your sister got drug into a fight because of us."

Back when the Yukon pack took Bailey, Kami had been put in the crossfire and kidnapped as well. She came out battered and bruised, but she fought through it.

Anger flashes in Tate's eyes. "As much as I hate what happened to her, in the end, she came out stronger."

"I wonder if it'll ever end. Will there ever be a time when I don't have to hide?" With people thinking I'm the last full-blooded royal arctic female, it helps the others not have a target on their heads. I trust Tate, but that knowledge is something I'll keep to myself for as long as I have to.

Tate stands next to me but keeps his distance. "It won't be like that forever, Faith. Look at your sister and Ryker, Cedric and Laila, and Tyla and Sebastian. They're happy and moving on with their lives. You'll get that chance one day."

By the way things are going, I doubt it. "I hope so," I say, trying to be positive. Taking a deep breath, I let it out slow and smile. "Shall we get to work? I'm ready to paint."

He nods toward the door. "Let's go."

We get in his truck and head on our way down his long, winding driveway. I look out the window toward the sun, loving the heat on my face. There's not a single cloud in the sky.

"Cedric tells me you and Micah started up your own land-scaping business. How's that going?"

"Pretty good while it lasted," I say, looking over at him. "Right now, he's on his own. I would do the garden work while he cut the grass."

He chuckles. "Planting flowers, huh? Most women I know don't like to get dirty."

He glances at me, and I shrug. "I don't mind it. Then again, I've trained with Micah my entire life. There were plenty of times I was thrown in the mud. Also, my mother was big into gardening. It's one of the things I remember about her. She was a Biology professor, so science was her life."

"And your dad? What did he do?" We turn onto the main road toward the small, quaint town of River Valley. It had an Old West feel to it when Colin and I drove through.

Thinking about him brings a smile to my face. "He was a doctor. The man was smarter than any person I know. I'm pretty sure he wanted me and my siblings to follow in his footsteps, but none of us got the chance."

"My dad's not a doctor, but I'm proud of everything he accomplished. The man can do just about anything."

I've heard stories about how his father stepped down as alpha so he could take his place. There are other packs out there that don't work like that. You have to fight for the right, even if it means taking out a family member.

We turn down a gravel road, and I can see a bright yellow country house in the distance. It reminds me of the yellow cottage Micah and I lived in. "How did your pack handle him stepping down and giving the position to you?" I ask.

Tate parks right in front of the house and looks over at me. "The Graysons have led the Great Plains pack for generations. It's how it's always been. No other families have challenged us."

Yet. I can't help but think that in my mind. Loyalty can be swayed if the price is right. Maybe I'm just jaded after everything my family's been through. It's better to expect the worst than to get blind-sided.

I nod toward the house. "This place is cute. Are the owners like us?"

We get out of the truck, and he shakes his head. "No, they're human. Recently married with a kid on the way. I was friends with them in high school, but they were a couple of years younger. They dated back then but broke up during college. As luck would have it, they recently found their way back to each other." He reaches into the back to grab some of the paint cans, and I help him by fetching the pans and brushes.

"That's a true love story there. Have many people in your pack found their mates?" I ask, following behind him up to the porch.

He slips the key into the lock. "Several have. I'm happy for them."

"What about you? Has anything happened between you and a female in your pack?" Yes, my curiosity has gotten the better of me. It shocks me that men like Chase and Tate haven't been claimed yet. There have to be tons of women who want them.

The door opens and he smirks. "Not yet. All of the women around my age in the pack are ones I grew up with. You'd think the mating signs would've already appeared."

"You never know," I say with a shrug. "Nothing about our kind makes sense. Things are always changing."

"That's for damn sure." He flourishes a hand inside, and I walk in. The house is light and airy with its cream-colored living room walls and country feel; it's perfect for a small family. "Anson and I painted the living room, the kitchen, and one of the bedrooms, but we still have one other bedroom and the nursery to finish."

As soon as the word nursery leaves his lips, that's where I want to go. "Which one is the nursery?"

Tate points down the small hallway. "It's the last room."

I've had so many ideas on decorating Cedric and Laila's nursery, but I didn't want to overstep. It's their baby's room and their house. When I get into the small bedroom, I look around at the navy-blue walls.

Tate leans against the doorframe with his arms crossed. "Jason and Anna are having a girl. They want this room light pink." When I think of little girls, I think of fairy gardens and magic.

An idea comes to mind, and I smile. "Since you're friends with this couple, how adventurous do you think they are?"

His brows furrowed with curiosity. "What do you have in mind?"

I glance around the room. "It's just an idea, but you have to trust me. Do you mind if I talk to them?"

Tate pulls out his cell and laughs. "Don't get me fired, Faith." He scrolls through his contacts and hands me the phone.

I press the call button and wink at him. "I won't. I promise."

ELEVEN

Anna was excited about my idea, but Tate has no clue what I'm doing. He took me to a local craft shop so we could purchase the supplies I needed. The hours went by quickly, but I was able to get the pink on the walls. Now it's ready for the fun stuff. I'm going to start on it first thing tomorrow when we go back to the house.

While Tate's outside on the phone talking to a client, I search through his refrigerator and cabinets and find that he has everything I need to make spaghetti. He also has all the ingredients I need for chocolate-covered peanut butter balls too, but I'll have to do them another time.

By the time Tate gets inside the house, the spaghetti sauce is done, and the noodles are almost ready. He walks into the kitchen with a shocked expression on his face. "Was I on the phone that long?"

I open one of the wine bottles Chase sent me for me. "Yep. But don't worry, I was going to eat without you."

Tate chuckles. "Hey, I'm fine with that. I appreciate you cooking."

"No problem," I say, taking a sip of the wine. "You sure do

have a lot of food in your refrigerator." His eyes twinkle mischievously at my comment. Pursing my lips, I stare at him, wondering what's going on in his mind. "Do you secretly know how to cook, and you're not telling me?"

He shrugs. "Maybe. I just never really have the time. I'm usually working from sunrise to sundown. Today is the first day I worked normal hours."

"Why do you work so much? Is it because you're bombarded with projects?"

His eyes freeze on mine, almost as if I caught him off guard with my question. He leans against the counter and looks away. "I guess it's because it's all I have. Besides the pack, work is my life."

There's a sadness to his tone, but what I can really sense is his need. He's trying to hold it back. Unmated males, especially alphas, feel the need a lot more than others. When it gets really bad, it's called the rage. Some wolves lose their minds from not finding their mates, and some get so violent there's no other choice but for them to be put down. I don't want to see that happen to Tate.

The noodles are done, so I drain them and put some on our plates. "I understand that, but you need to enjoy life. You have the whole world at your fingertips. I'd give anything to have the freedom you have."

I pour the meat sauce over his noodles and hand it to him. He nods toward the back door. "Want to eat outside on the patio?" He goes to the refrigerator and pulls out a beer.

"Sure." I fix my plate, and he opens the door for me. His backyard is gorgeous with a brick patio and pool, surrounded by twinkling lights.

"Kami put up the lights," he informs me with a laugh. "I couldn't say no to her."

Grinning, I glance back at him. "I had a feeling. I do love the lights though. It's something I would've done too."

We set our plates down on the patio table. Tate waves a hand around his yard. "What else would you do out here? You're the landscaping expert."

I roll my eyes. "Oh, whatever. I'm not an expert. However, I do love color, and that's what you're missing." His patio and pool are just there with nothing around them, no shrubberies or trees for privacy. He already has privacy with him living alone on the mountaintop, but aesthetically, his yard could use more. I get up and walk around the pool. "To create a barrier around the pool, I could plant some zebra grass. It comes in a variety of colors, so it'll be a good contrast with the water."

Tate leans back in his chair. "I like that. What else?"

"You could always add some Crassula and Yucca as well. They have a rich, green color, and they're good for filling in the spaces."

His grin widens, and it makes my heart race. "When do you want to get started?"

I walk back over to him. "You're hiring me?"

Chuckling, he opens his beer. "If you want the job."

"I guess it depends on if I have time," I say, laughing. "I'm kind of busy on another job."

He turns up his beer and sighs. "True. And you only have six days left here. It might have to wait until you come back."

It makes me wonder if I will. There's no telling what's going to happen between now and the next few weeks. I focus on my spaghetti and twirl the noodles around my fork. "If I don't get to come back, I can always tell you what you need. It's pretty simple." I look out at the pool. "Besides the zebra grass and the others, you could add some hydrangeas and maybe some small dwarf-sized fruit trees. That way, you'll get fruit and color added to your yard." I eat my bite of spaghetti, wondering what else could be done.

Out of the corner of my eye, I can see Tate staring at me. The blood races through my body, and I can feel the heat in my cheeks. When I look at him, his lips pull back slowly into a sexy smirk. "I'm glad you're here, Faith. I've really enjoyed your company."

"Likewise."

"Where do you go next?"

I blow out a sigh. "To Ian's."

His smile disappears, and he looks away. "Randale's a good guy."

"He's a little intense," I say, wondering if he'll say more. "He doesn't seem to be as playful-natured as you and Chase."

He snorts. "That's because he's not. Ian's had to fight hard for what he has. When he was eight years old, he watched his father get defeated in combat by another wolf who became their pack's alpha. By the time he was fifteen, he'd had enough. He defeated the alpha, and no one has challenged him since." Tate brings the beer to his lips. "I can see why he is the way he is."

I can see it too. "I'm curious to see what it'll be like with him next week."

Tate sets his beer down, his gaze serious. "How did you come up with your plan anyway? Honestly, I'm shocked it's even something you would do."

"Why is that?"

He shrugs. "You're an unmated royal female, Faith. Yes, Ian, Colton, Chase, and I are allies to the Teton pack, but we're still men. You know the troubles we face, and yet, you're here."

Do I tell him the truth? I don't think I've fully admitted it to myself. I lift my gaze to the darkening sky, finding strength within the moon and stars. I feel like I can tell Tate anything. He may not be my mate, but there's a connection between us.

"As I said to you inside, I'd give anything to have your freedom." I tear my gaze away from the sky to look at him. "With Killian trying to take me, my only option was to get away.

Micah would never let me go alone, so I had to think of another plan. You and Chase came to mind. Cedric is a dear friend of mine, and I feel connected to you and Chase as I do with him. He's a dear friend, and I trust him with my life."

"And you feel that way with me?" he asks.

I nod. "I do. That's why I knew this plan would work. Now don't get me wrong, I've wondered about Ian and Colton since I don't know them that well, but I figured I'd give it a try."

"What if you don't like being with them?"

I've thought about that, and it worries me. I might be hating my plan once it's all said and done. "I don't know," I answer, really not knowing what I would do." Closing my eyes, I cover my face with my hands. "Okay, fine. You want the full truth?" When I look at him, he nods. I can feel the burn of embarrassment on my cheeks. "I was hoping to find my mate."

Tate sits back, his gaze serious. "And you thought visiting the other packs would help?"

I shrug. "It's a start. All I know is that he's not in the Teton pack. If I don't get out and meet other people, I'll never find him."

He focuses on his spaghetti. "I understand, Faith. You're not the only one who thinks their mate is somewhere else."

Silence fills the air as we finish our dinner. I look up at the moon and send up a silent prayer. If I were to pick a mate, I'd want it to be someone like Tate. Even though I feel a connection to him, it's obvious it's not going to happen for us. One day, I hope he finds his happiness too.

TWELVE

I never thought I'd want someone as bad as I want Faith. Ever since she came to my home, she's all I've been able to think about. What's fucked up is that I shouldn't be having these thoughts about her. She's not my mate. The only time I can think of something else is when I'm working. That's why I made it a point to get to our job early. Faith is in the nursery, and I'm across the house with Anson, replacing the flooring. It's been hours, and we're almost done, which means the second I see Faith, all of the feelings I have for her will hit me once more.

"So ... I was thinking."

I grab up the last of my tools and look over at Anson. "Thinking about what?"

Anson clears his throat and nods toward the door, keeping his voice low. "Let's go outside." I walk past him, and he follows me out to the truck. Whatever he has to say, I guess he doesn't want Faith hearing.

When we get outside, I place all of my tools in the back of the truck. "What's going on?" I ask.

Anson glances back at the house and then at me. "I think you should tell the pack Faith is here."

The words *hell no* are on the tip of my tongue, but I hold them back. A sense of protectiveness overwhelms me, and I can't shake it. It's something I've never felt before. I don't want Faith anywhere near the men in our pack.

"We're trying to keep her hidden," I say.

Anson nods. "I know, but what if her mate is someone in our pack. This could be their chance to find happiness."

I shake my head. "She's been around all of us before. It would've happened already." That's what pisses me off more than anything. Faith is an amazing woman, and it's obvious there's something between us. I know she feels it just as I do. I've known plenty of wolves who have fallen in love with humans. Unfortunately, this is a little more complicated than that.

Anson lowers his voice. "That's not true, and you know it. It can take time."

Anger wells up in my chest. "I said no. We're not going to dangle her around like a piece of meat."

"What if she's up for it?"

Clenching my teeth, I meet his gaze. I don't want to get angry, but I know what he wants. He wants to get close to Faith, to see if she could be his. I refuse to share her with anyone. "It's not going to happen. End of discussion."

Anson huffs. "Fine. I'm calling it a day." He storms over to his truck and drives away.

I look over at the nursery window, and I can see Faith inside, smiling as she focuses on the wall. I can't see what she's done, but I have no doubt it's impressive. Now that Anson's gone, a part of me regrets how I handled our conversation. What he said was right, and I know it. The magic of the moon doesn't always work instantaneously. My parents grew up together, and their mating signs didn't appear until they were twenty-three years old. One night they happened to run into each other in the woods after a run, and it just happened. It seems so simple, but it's not.

Faith moves out of sight, and it's not long before she comes out the back door. "Hey," she says, grinning excitedly. Her smile is so damn beautiful. It takes all I have to control my thoughts and emotions around her. I know she can sense my need at times, but it's only because I lost my focus. It's so hard to concentrate around her. She walks down the patio stairs and comes over to me. "The nursery's almost done. I should have it finished tomorrow."

I lean against my truck. "Great. I'll have all of my stuff done too. Jason and Anna will be happy to know they can move in a few days early."

She glances over her shoulder at the house. "I hope Anna likes what I did."

"I'm sure she will."

Eyes narrowed, she looks at me. "You haven't even seen it."

"True," I say, laughing, "but I trust you."

She beams. "You should. I'm not going to disappoint you."

"I never thought you would." I nod toward the truck. "Come on, let's get out of here." We get in my car and head back to my house. She's been in my protection for three days, and I'm already dreading her leaving. I don't know why I feel so protective of Faith when she's not even mine.

My wolf stirs inside of me, desperate to find his mate.

Why is it we always want something we can't have?

THIRTEEN

FAITH

After Tate and I finished dinner, I helped him clean up the kitchen and then retreated to my room to make my daily phone calls. Bailey informed me that Asher has a tooth coming in. I hate I can't be there to see it. There have been no more sightings of Killian and his men, according to Cedric and Laila. It makes me wonder how long they're going to search for me. Will they ever give up? The only way for that to happen is for me to find my mate. I'll be useless to them once I do. My mate and I will be stronger than Killian and his witch once we're bonded. If Laila hadn't told us that, I never would've known.

Sitting on the bed, I lean against the headboard and scroll to Micah's name on my phone. I always save him for last since I talk to him the most. I press send, and it rings only once before I hear his voice.

"Hey," he answers.

"Hey. Did you have a good day?"

He chuckles. "I did. Amelie and I trained this morning. She's gotten so much stronger. The woman loves to give me hell."

I burst out laughing. "She's making up for the hell I'm not there to give you."

"Yeah, I think you might be right. I like it, though. She has fire." They would make a perfect match, but they haven't shown any of the mating signs. I hear a splash outside and walk over to the side window in my room. When I look out, I see Tate swimming around in the pool, his smooth skin glistening in the water. My heart races and my body tightens in all the right places.

"Faith, you still there?"

"Yes." I quickly move away from the window, hoping like hell Tate didn't catch me watching him. "Sorry."

"You okay?" he asks.

"I'm fine. Just got a little distracted." I clear my throat, trying to think of something quick to say. "Tate and I are almost done with the house I was telling you about. The nursery is so cute. I'll send you pictures when I get done tomorrow." I look over at the window, wishing I could peek through the curtains.

"Nice. I can't wait to see it."

We talk for a few more minutes, and then we say our goodbyes. I set my phone down on the nightstand and slowly creep over to the window. Tate is still in the pool, swimming laps. I have the strongest urge to go down there and join him. But do I? I have a bikini packed with my things, but I feel like I'll just be adding fuel to the flames. Do I want to stoke the fire? As exciting as it sounds, it's best I don't. It's not fair to either one of us, especially not Tate. The last thing I need to do is flaunt my body in front of him. So instead, I'll go down there in my denim shorts and paint-covered T-shirt.

Once downstairs, I slip out the back door. Tate is still swimming laps and hasn't noticed me yet. I stop at the edge of the pool, right by the diving board. Tate swims toward me and stops at the edge, lifting his head out of the water.

He swipes a hand over his face and smiles up at me. "Hey. I didn't know you were going to come out here."

I shrug. "I finished my phone calls early. Thought I'd enjoy the night air." I flourish a hand about the pool. "Do you swim a lot?"

Still looking up at me, he rests his arms over the edge. "All the time. You should jump in.

"That's okay," I say, laughing as I glance down at my clothes. "I didn't bring a swimsuit." Total lie, but it's all I can think of to get out of swimming.

A wolfish grin spreads across his face. "Oh, you don't need a bathing suit." I don't have time to react before he grabs my legs and tosses me into the pool. The water muffles my screams.

I surface fast splash him in the face. "You're such an asshole."

He splashes me back, and a water war ensues. "You should've known better than to stand near the edge."

Laughing, I charge after him and push him under. He reaches around me and takes me with him. His deep laugh echoes under the water, and I smile. I don't want to fight against him with his arms around me, but I can't let him know how good it feels. Pushing him away, I swim over to the edge, and he does the same, only leaving about two feet between us. He looks at me and laughs, and I splash him one more time.

"I'll pay you back for this," I tell him.

He winks. "I look forward to it." We stare at each other for a few seconds, and then his expression turns serious. "There's something I want to talk to you about."

My heart stops, and I hold my breath. "What is it?"

His eyes flash to his wolf's, and when he closes and opens them back up, they're his usual bright blue. "Anson asked me today if I'd let you spend time with the other males in the pack."

Taking a deep breath, I let it out slowly. "And what did you say?"

He looks away. "I told him no."

Heart racing, I freeze. When his eyes meet mine, it's like he can sense how much I want him. His need washes over me, drawing me closer. "Why did you say no?"

This time, he's the one who swims closer. We're now only a foot apart. "I said no because I don't want to share you. But then, it's not my place to deny you. If you wish to spend time with my pack, I won't stop you." Mouth gaping, I can't find the words to say. He moves closer, and we're only a breath apart. I can feel the heat from his lips. "I wish you knew how fucking bad I want you as my mate. Your face is all I see when I close my eyes at night." I want to kiss him, but he swims away and gets out of the pool. His swim shorts ride low on his hips, and I can't hide my attraction to him. Even the cool water can't ease off the heat of my skin. He picks up his towel and runs it over his face. "I can sense what your body does around me. It drives me crazy not to act on it." Still keeping his back to me, he turns his head to the side but doesn't fully look at me. "What kind of mate do you want, Faith?"

I don't want to lie to him. Climbing out of the pool, I walk over to him, but he still keeps his back to me. "If I had my choice, I'd want someone like you." A few seconds pass, and I resist the urge to touch him. It gets harder and harder the longer I'm around him.

FOURTEEN

FAITH

I get up early to make breakfast for Tate and me, but he beat me to it. When I walk into the kitchen, there's a pan of eggs, a plate full of bacon, and a pile of banana pancakes. Tate walks in—looking unbelievably sexy in his jeans and a tight gray T-shirt—and there's no denying the sexual tension between us, especially after what happened last night.

His eyes meet mine. "Faith, I ..."

Before he can finish, the front door opens. "Good morning!" Kami walks in and smiles, her eyes darting back and forth from me to Tate. "It smells amazing in here."

Tate nods toward the food. "I made plenty. Dig in."

Her stomach growls. "Don't mind if I do. I was going to see if you both wanted to go to Granny's café for breakfast, but it doesn't look like we need to do that."

Tate pours himself some coffee. "Nope. You two enjoy it. I'll be outside making some phone calls." Then to me, he says, "After you eat, we'll head to Jason and Anna's."

I grab another plate out of the cabinet for Kami. "Sounds good."

As soon as he walks out, Kami rushes over to me. "What the hell is going on here? There is some serious sexual tension."

Groaning, I hang my head in my hands. "Tate and I kind of had a moment last night."

Her mouth drops open. "What kind of moment? Did you two sleep together?"

"No," I gasp. Then again, the thought has crossed my mind, and I did dream about us having sex last night. I spoon a bundle of eggs onto my plate, along with a couple of pieces of bacon.

Kami does the same but waves her hand in the air for me to continue. "Explain. You can't leave me like that."

I pile two pancakes on top of my eggs and sit down at the kitchen table. "I'm starting to have feelings for your brother."

She sets her plate down and slowly lowers into the seat across from me. "Seriously?" All smiles are gone.

"Yeah," I reply.

"And let me guess, no mating signs yet?"

I shake my head. "Nope. Do you see the dilemma?"

With a heavy sigh, she takes a bite of her food. "This sucks ass, Faith. You and Tate would be perfect for each other."

He's everything I could ever want in a mate. I wish we could make the choice for ourselves. "I guess it's just not meant to be."

Kami huffs. "I don't get it."

"Don't get what?" Anson asks as he strolls into the kitchen. I didn't even hear him walk through the door. As far as second-in-command's go, he's similarly built to Tate with his height and muscular body.

Kami bats her eyelashes at him in a sarcastic way. "I don't get why you think it's okay to walk in without knocking."

He drapes his arm over her shoulders and winks at her. "Because I can."

Kami shakes him off. "Men."

Anson glances at us both. "Where's Grayson? He told me to meet him at nine at Jason and Anna's, but I thought I'd stop by here first."

Kami snorts. "I wonder why," she says, mumbling under her breath.

Anson understood her and turned his eyes to me, but I quickly focus on my plate of food, pretending I didn't hear anything. Tate walks in, and my gaze instantly lifts to him.

"Hey, man," he says to Anson. "I thought you were meeting us at the house?"

Anson opens his mouth to speak, but Tate's phone rings, interrupting him. Tate stares down at the screen, his gaze narrowed. "I'll be right back." He walks into the living room and answers the phone. A few seconds later, he comes back and grabs his truck keys off the counter. "It was the lumber warehouse," he says to Anson. "There was an issue with one of our orders."

Tate peers down at my plate and over at Kami, clearly in a hurry to leave but too polite to tell me to eat quickly. "Go," I say. "Anson's going to the house so he can give me a ride."

Anson nods. "I'll be happy to take her."

Tate's jaw clenches, but he agrees. "Okay."

Kami raises her hand. "I'll go too. I can help Faith finish up the nursery. That way, she's not spending her entire week with us working."

Tate shrugs. "I told her we didn't have to."

I hold up my hands. "I didn't want you all putting your lives on hold because I'm here." To Tate, I wave him toward the door. "Go. We'll see you soon."

Turning on his heel, he gives Anson a warning stare, which is definitely an alpha move. His words replay in my head about him not wanting to share me. Shivers run down my skin, and I smile. I find it sexy as hell. Kami grins at me, but we straighten up when Anson turns back to us.

"Guess we'll go when you two are ready."

"It won't take long," I say, eating a bite of my banana pancake. I've never had them before, and it's delicious.

Kami snickers. "They're good, aren't they?"

"Yes," I gush, savoring the next bite. "I'll have to tell your brother so."

Anson sits down beside Kami. "How are you liking it here?" he asks me.

I nod. "I love it. It's been nice getting away on my own for a change. There's so much I haven't seen and so many places I haven't been."

"What will you do when it's safe to go home? Will you go back or head out and explore the world?"

"I don't know," I say, glancing down at my food. "I'll have to figure that out when the time comes. Something tells me I'll never be safe until I find my mate." The room falls silent, and I use this time to finish eating. Kami helps me clean the dishes, and when we're done, she hops into the back seat, leaving me to sit up front with Anson.

I look over at him, and he smiles as he starts up the truck. "How did you get that scar?" I ask him.

He rubs a finger over his right eyebrow. "It happened the night we helped rescue your sister from the Yukon pack. It was a wolfsbane laced dagger."

It's not common for a shifter's skin to scar, but it does happen if wolfsbane is involved. I remember that night very well, even though I was far away. "Thank you for helping save her. I knew what was going on, but Micah refused to let me get anywhere near Wyoming. I had never felt so helpless in my life."

He sighs. "And now people are after you. Does it make you wish you weren't a royal?"

"No," I say in all seriousness. "I'm happy with who I am and where I came from."

"Besides Tyla and Sebastian's baby girl, are there more royal arctic females in the world?"

I've been waiting on someone to ask this question, and my answer will always be the same. "No. I'm the last full-blooded royal arctic." Tyla and Sebastian's daughter is half arctic and half gray, but she's still a royal because of Sebastian's blood. Right now, she's not in any danger, but I have no clue what it'll be like when she gets older.

When we pull up to Jason and Anna's house, Tate's truck isn't there. Kami pats my shoulder and opens her door. "Come on. I'm dying to see what you've done." I jump out of the truck, and we go inside. The nursery door is closed, and when I open it, Kami's mouth drops. "Wow. This is absolutely magical."

I wink at her. "That's exactly what I was going for."

My heart races as I watch Jason and Anna walk up the front porch stairs to the door. Their house is done, and even though I only contributed to the nursery, I'm excited to see what they think of everything. Tate and Anson worked hard on finishing the house. They meet the young couple outside and point out everything they did to the exterior.

Seeing Tate smile brings a smile to my face. I've enjoyed watching him work and how he takes pride in what he does. Kami stands by my side and gently nudges me. "You know, you don't need magic to tell who your mate is. If you and my brother have feelings for each other, you shouldn't ignore them."

"You know it doesn't work like that."

Crossing her arms over her chest, she stands in front of me, blocking my view of Tate. There's a seriousness to her I've never seen before. "Who says it doesn't? We've all been waiting to find our true mates, but I say we go out and find them ourselves. Why can't we?"

Her passion is what I love most about her. She reminds me a lot of Tate. It makes me wonder if people see similarities between me and Colin and Bailey. I would hope so because they're two of the strongest people I know.

Kami steps out of the way just as Tate leads Jason and Anna to the front door with Anson following behind them. She makes a valid point. Why can't we mate with who we fall in love with? The answer is simple ... we can.

"You're right, Kami. We should be able to make the choice."

Her eyes light up. "What are you going to do?" Tate and the others walk in.

I lean in close to whisper in her ear. "I'm not sure yet, but I'll figure it out."

Jason and Anna already know Anson and Kami, so Tate introduces them to me. I shake their hands and walk with them through the house as Tate shows them everything. My nerves are shot. Anna wanted to save the nursery for last. I'm dying for her to see it, but I'm also afraid she'll hate what I did. I may have overdone it a little.

My palms grow sweaty the closer we get to the nursery. Tate stops at the door and smiles at me. "Do you want to open it?"

Taking a deep breath, I let it out slowly. "Okay." I walk over to the door and stand next to him.

Anna bounces on her feet excitedly. "I can't wait to see this."

Jason chuckles and squeezes her shoulders. "You're gonna make the baby pop out early jumping around like that."

Kami bursts out laughing. "I don't think it works like that, Jason."

He shrugs. "Hey, it could. You never know. Back in the day, they put pregnant women in confinement so excitement wouldn't make them go into early labor."

I nod. "That's true, especially with the royals. How did you know that?"

Anna snickers and pats him on the stomach. "He's a huge Tudors fan. I think we watched the show a gazillion times." I haven't watched the show, but I had plenty of time to read as a kid.

Placing my hand on the doorknob, I slowly turn it. "All right, here we go." When I open the door, I step aside so Jason and Anna can walk in first. What used to be a navy-blue room has completely transformed into a magical faerie garden. The ceiling is a bright blue with dreamy white clouds. It almost feels as if you're outside. The rest of the room is where the magic is. There are flowers and grass painted on three of the walls, and the rolling hills behind that make it look like the faerie land keeps going on and on for miles. On the final wall, I painted a serene lake with a gazebo covered in an array of rainbow pastel flowers.

Anna clasps her hands over her mouth and circles around, her eyes instantly filling with tears. "Oh. My. God. This is ..."

Kami is the one bouncing around now. "Isn't it amazing? When I walked in here yesterday, I couldn't believe my eyes."

Anna walks over to the wall and grazes a hand over the flowers. "It's exquisite. I don't know of anyone who can do this kind of painting."

I look over at Tate, and he's just as shocked by the look of awe on his face. He turns to me and lifts his hands in the air. "Why didn't you tell me you could do stuff like this?"

I shrug. "I didn't want to toot my own horn."

Kami snorts. "I would be if I had this kind of talent."

Anna opens her arms and pulls me in for a hug. "Thank you for this, Faith. I'm starting to think I want this room for myself." She lets me go and laughs. "When people find out about this, you'll be swamped with work. I have so many friends who'd love something like this painted in their homes."

"Unfortunately," Tate cuts in, "Faith's only here for a few more days."

Anna frowns. "That's a bummer. If that changes and you find yourself back here, let me know. I know some people who'll pay big bucks for your work."

I wink at her. "I'll be sure to call you."

Jason asks Tate and Anson to show him the rest of the house again, so they leave the room along with Kami. Anna circles around, and I love how it feels to see people admire my work. A piece of my soul goes into every painting I paint.

"Where did you get the inspiration for this?" Anna asks.

If I told her, she wouldn't believe me. It came from Laila's journals her fae mother had written. Only a thin veil separates the fae world and the mortal realm. Laila's mother lived in both places. In her journals, she described the Land of the Fae with such detail that I could see it as clear as day in my mind. I've been waiting for a chance to paint it, and what better way than for it to be in a little girl's room.

I smile at Anna. "It came from a book I read."

She giggles. "I'm starting to think I want to live in that book."

No one other than the fae can cross into the Land of the Fae. If I had the chance, I'd go there in a heartbeat. "Me too," I say in all seriousness. "It would be an enchanting place indeed."

FIFTEEN

TATE

Jason shakes my hand and then Anson's. "I appreciate your hard work, guys."

I slap his shoulder. "You're welcome."

He sighs and focuses back on the house. Anna is still in the nursery talking to Faith. "I haven't seen my wife this excited about anything in a long time."

Anson chuckles. "Then you must be doing something wrong."

We all laugh, and Kami shakes her head. "I don't want to hear about that."

Jason pats me on the arm. "All right, let me go in and get Anna before she talks Faith's ears off." He disappears inside.

"You ready to go?" I ask Kami.

"Actually," she says, turning to Anson. "I was hoping you could give me a ride home?"

Anson shrugs. "Sure. I'm ready when you are."

She grins wide. "Give me just one sec. I need to talk to Tate for a minute."

Anson pats my back and nods toward his truck. "I'll be in

the truck." Then to me, he lifts his brows. "We working tomorrow?"

I shake my head. "Nope. I'm taking a break."

He smiles. "Sounds good to me."

Faith watches him walk away and waves her hand impatiently for him to hurry, even though he can't see what she's doing. "Are you okay?"

She moves closer. "Yeah, I want to talk to you before Faith gets out here."

"What's going on?"

Her voice lowers. "Do you have feelings for her?"

Taken aback, I stare at her, wondering why she'd even ask. Did Faith say something? "Why do you want to know?"

"Because," she says quickly. "Faith has feelings for you; she told me she did. You know my views on this. I think it's screwed up how we have to wait for our mate to come along. Why can't we love who we want to love?"

"What do you suggest we do? Act on it?"

Her eyes glow, and she stands firm. "Yes. You and Faith are perfect for each other. I think you'd be stupid to let her go." Jason and Anna walk out of the house, and so does Faith. Kami grabs my arm, drawing my attention back to her. "Talk to her, Tate. I don't want to see you give up on this. To hell with the rules. If she cares for you and you care for her, nothing should stand in your way."

Could it really be that simple? The only problem is that it goes against everything we've known. Yes, some complete the bond when they're not true mates, and they'll never be fully happy. I don't want that, but I also don't want to let Faith go.

"Okay," I say, lowering my voice. "I'll talk to her."

Kami beams. "Great. I'll let you two enjoy your ride home." She turns around and says goodbye to Faith before hurrying over to Anson's truck.

Faith chuckles. "She's mighty happy right now. Is there something going on between her and Anson?"

Laughing, I open up her door. "Definitely, not. He's like the annoying brother to her."

"And you're not?" she teases.

"Nah. I'm the cool one."

She hops in, and I shut the door. It feels good to banter back and forth with her. There's still a lot of tension between us, so much uncertainty and confusion. I want her, and there's no denying it. But if I tell her, what will it do to us? She's a friend, and I don't want to jeopardize that.

We start on our way to the house, and Faith's stomach growls. She covers her stomach and giggles. "I must be hungry."

It just so happens that we drive past one of my favorite restaurants on the way to my house. "I know a good place we can get takeout. Their special tonight is buttermilk fried chicken, garlic mashed potatoes, and green beans."

Her eyes light up. "Oh yeah? I'm good with that. If I had more of your banana pancakes, I'd be stuffing them in my mouth right now."

That makes me feel good. "Did you like them?"

She nods. "They were heaven. You'll have to make them again."

"I can do that."

I pull into the parking lot of the small mom-and-pop restaurant my parents used to take me to ever since I was a little boy. The older couple who owns it are both in their eighties and still going strong. With my parents still looking young, they often confuse my father for me. That's one of the things we have to be careful about. We live in a small town, and most of the humans my parents knew when they were younger are dead now.

Faith and I walk inside and order our food. We wait for only a few minutes, and then we're back on the road, food in hand. When we get to the house, I set the food on the table, and Faith grabs two beers out of the refrigerator.

I lift my brows at her. "No wine tonight?"

She shrugs. "I'm in a beer mood."

So am I. I need it if I'm going to do what I'm about to do. Hell, I need a whole case. We sit down at the table and eat. I have no doubt she can hear my heart thumping wildly. Hers is doing the same, which doesn't help matters. Every time I try to speak, I can't form the words. What I really want to do is pull her into my arms and say that I want her so fucking bad that I'd give up everything just to have her. Even my wolf wants to claim her, and I've never had him be so restless before. That last thing I want is to scare her away, or worse, cause a rift between my pack and hers.

"I can't believe you never told me you painted," I say, trying to get my thoughts back to reality. "What you did at Jason and Anna's was pretty epic."

She looks away and smiles. "Thanks. I actually sell some of my work in one of the local galleries at home."

I'm impressed but definitely not surprised; she's very talented. "I'm happy for you, Faith. You're a woman of many talents. What else is going on in your life you haven't told me about?"

"Well," she replies, drawing out the word, "not only do I paint and do landscaping, but I also just got hired to be the art teacher at our elementary school."

I can see her working with kids. She has that sweetness about her that I know children will be drawn to. "I'm happy for you, Faith."

"Thanks." We stare at each other for a few seconds, but then she jerks her gaze away and gets up to throw her to-go box away. She goes over to my kitchen cabinets and pulls out my peanut butter and powdered sugar. "I was thinking of making chocolate-covered peanut butter balls. Is that okay?" Her heart races even more, and I can tell she's intentionally keeping her back to me.

I toss my box into the trash and slowly close the distance between us. I can't wait any longer. "Faith, look at me." A sigh escapes her lips, and she slowly turns around. I step closer, and she lifts her gaze to mine. "What are we doing?"

"I don't know," she whispers. "All I know is that I feel things for you. I want things I can't have."

My hands ache to touch her, but I keep them to myself. "Who says you can't?"

She laughs, but there's no humor to it. "Life. But then, someone brought up a valid point to me today. She said we should be able to choose our path, make our own choices."

Kami.

"And do you think she's right?"

Her eyes drop down to my lips. "I want her to be."

"So do I," I agree.

Her breath hitches and she meets my gaze. "What are we going to do?"

Taking her hands, I pull her closer, but I don't kiss her even though it's what I really want to do. "You're here for three more days. I say we go out and enjoy life, just you and me. My family has a cabin near Yellowstone. We can stay there, and I can take you to see Old Faithful, the waterfalls, and whatever else you want."

She squeezes my hands. "I'd like that."

As much as it kills me, I slowly let her go and step back. "We'll leave out first thing in the morning." The need in her rises, and it takes all I have not to take her on the kitchen table. I nod toward the stairs. "I think I'm going to turn in for the night." What I need is a fucking cold shower. "If you need anything, you know where to find me."

She nods. "See you in the morning."

Turning on my heel, I walk away from her. It gets harder and harder each time.

SIXTEEN

FAITH

I've been staying alone with Tate in his house, but something feels different about being alone with him in his family's cabin. I'm excited yet terrified all at the same time. Last night, he couldn't get away from me fast enough. I could feel the need soaring in my body. He showed incredible restraint, and I doubt any other wolf would've been able to do the same. I always thought I had stellar self-control, but I'm starting to question it.

We left early this morning before sunrise to head to Yellowstone National Park. We entered through the West Entrance and started at Gibbon Falls before working our way to the Lower Falls and Upper Falls. I've never seen anything so beautiful in my life. There are many tourists with it being summer, but it doesn't take the magic away.

There were tons of bison walking around, and I made sure to take loads of pictures. I want to remember everything about the day. Tate and I have talked non-stop, but nothing has been said about *us*. I know what it does to him when we do. Hell, I'm starting to think it affects me more than him. I'm the one who feels like I'll lose control if things get heated between us.

We drive past Yellowstone Lake with all the snow-capped mountains in the background. Then we stop by Old Faithful to watch it explode amongst the hundreds of tourists around us. I've never heard so many *ooohs* and *ahhhs* in my life; it took all I had not to laugh. After that, we visited all the different basins and walked around on the wooden pathways.

By the end of the day, my mind is full of everything we've seen. The sun dips behind the mountains, giving the sky a pinkish glow. Tate starts up the truck, and we head on our way out of the park.

"Did you have fun?" he asks, sneaking a glance my way.

Rolling the window down, I close my eyes as the wind blows through my hair. "I had a lot of fun," I reply.

"It would be the perfect night for a run, but I know you can't right now. There's a lake not far from the cabin."

I look over at him and brush the hair out of my face. "We can still go for a run. I just can't shift."

He nods. "Does that not bother you?"

Reaching into my pocket, I pull out the black carmine stone. If I shift, there will be no way to keep it on my body, not unless I put it in my mouth. Knowing my luck, I'd swallow it. "It sucks, but it's what I have to do to stay hidden." I slide it back into my pocket. "I'd still like to go for a run. I bet I can beat you to that lake even if you run as your wolf."

He smirks. "Deal."

It's dark by the time we pull down the dark gravel road toward the cabin. When we get there, it's not at all like I expected; it's even better. The place is small and quaint, with rocking chairs on the front porch. Tate reaches into the backseat and grabs our bags.

"You ready?"

I nod and get out of the truck. When we go inside, it's rustic but with a lot of charm. Tate nods toward the hallway where there are two bedrooms and one bathroom. He opens the door to one of the bedrooms and sets my bag on the queen-sized bed.

"How often do you come up here?" I ask.

Tate sighs and peers around the room. "It's been a while. You should've seen this place when we bought it. It was a disaster. My dad and I redid everything." I love how involved he is with his family. I'd give anything to have that kind of time with mine.

"I'd love to meet your parents."

His smile makes everything inside of me tighten. "I'm sure they'd love that." He turns to the window and nods. "Ready for that run?"

There's a new moon tonight. Only royals and the strongest of our kind can shift when the sky is black. He's never told me if he's one of the ones who can or not. I'm curious to find out.

"Let's go." Sliding a hand over my pocket, I can feel the stone safely tucked inside. Tate opens the front door, and I slip past him onto the porch. "So which way is the lake? I have to know since I'll be in the lead," I say, giggling at my joke.

Tate takes off his shirt and points toward the north. "We'll go straight through that way, and when we get to the small waterfall, veer left. The lake will be a half-mile further."

Bending down, I stretch my leg muscles and watch him curiously as he unzips his jeans. "Are you shifting tonight?"

His eyes flash, and he gives me a wolfish grin. "Should I not?"

I look up at the sky. "There's no moon tonight."

Chuckling, he drops his jeans to the ground, showing off his magnificent bare body. "That's never stopped me."

"Oh yeah? I'd like to see this."

He stalks toward me. "Do you not think I'm strong enough."

The breath hitches in my lungs as his power unleashes all around me. It almost knocks me off my feet. I've never felt that kind of strength from him before. Yes, he's an alpha, but it's like he kept this wilder, stronger side of him a secret.

"What is this?" I say, my voice breathless.

His eyes glow as he stares into mine. "I'm showing you who I really am."

I fight the urge to touch him. "You're a lot stronger than you let on. Why do you hide it?"

He smirks. "I like it that way; it gives me an advantage."

"A modest wolf. I'm not surprised in the least." Tate has never been one to flaunt anything. That's what I liked about him from the very beginning. He's not arrogant. I step out of his way and flourish a hand toward the woods. "Are we ready?" His grin widens, and he closes his eyes as his body shimmers, transforming him into his wolf. Alphas are always larger than the rest of his pack, and Tate is a massive gray. My wolf grows restless inside of me, desperate for a run. I'll be glad when I don't have to hide anymore.

Tate shakes out his fur and stretches. It's cute, and I can't help but smile. When he growls, I throw my hands up and laugh. "Sorry. I've never seen you like this before." I stretch my arms over my head and crack my neck. "I'm ready when you are." He stands next to me, but I keep my eyes on the direction I have to go. "On three. One. Two. Three." We both take off at the same time, dodging through the trees in a blur. The warm forest floor feels sensational against my bare feet, but it makes me miss being a wolf even more. I breathe in the scent of the woods, the air, and everything all around me; it's heaven.

The sound of rushing water grows closer, and up ahead, I see the small waterfall. I veer off to the left and push my legs as fast as they can go. Tate's right beside me, but I refuse to let him beat me. I may not be strong enough to outmatch him or any other alpha in combat, but I can do some damage. As far as running, there's no doubt about it ... I'm faster.

The lake is up ahead, and I push myself harder than I've

ever done in my life. Tate showed me his true self, and it's time I show him what I'm capable of. I shoot past him, my muscles burning like fire. He huffs and puffs to catch up to me, but it's no use. I won.

When I get to the lake, my feet slide against the sand, and I fall onto my back, my chest rising and falling with my rapid breaths. Tate hovers over me and growls, and all I do is laugh.

"I won. Bet you didn't think I was that fast, huh?" He sits down on his haunches beside me, giving me a wolfish grin with his tongue lolling out to the side. I sit up and gaze out at the lake. "If there's one thing Micah taught me, it was to be fast; to push my body to the limits. I might not be able to win a fight against a stronger wolf, but if I can outrun him, that's all that matters."

Tate's wolf shimmers away as he takes his human form. "You're right. I'm impressed with how fast you are. Micah trained you well. I think Kami could use that kind of help."

I get to my feet and walk over to the water's edge. An idea pops into my head. "What if I were to train her?" I say.

Tate's eyes widen. "You'd do that?"

When I look at him, my eyes instantly wander down to a certain appendage between his legs. "I, uh ..." So many things run through my mind, most of them involving a dream I had of us together in bed, his body draped over mine. I lift my gaze to his, and by the devilish smirk on his face, it's like he knows what I'm thinking.

Tate chuckles and gets to his feet. "What's wrong? Tongue-tied?"

Crossing my arms over my chest, I glare at him. "Smart ass. But yes, I'd be happy to train Kami. I don't know how or when, but we'll make it happen."

He takes a step toward me, and I walk back into the water. "What's on your mind, Faith? I want to hear it." There's nothing but seriousness on his face, and it makes me tremble. Maybe I should come right out and tell him how much I want him. It doesn't change the fact that we're not mates.

Heart racing, I can feel the heat rise to my cheeks. I take another step into the water, and my foot slides across a rock, making me lose balance. Tate reaches out to help, but he gets sucked in and plunges into the water with me. We both burst out laughing, and he takes my hands to help me up.

Instead of letting me go, he pulls me in close to his body. All playfulness aside, he stares down at me, his gaze heat-filled and raw. His cock hardens between his legs, and he presses it against me. "I know I shouldn't, but I want you so fucking bad. It kills me to let you go to another man."

I slide my hands out of his and glide them up to his wet chest. "I don't want to go either."

He cups my cheeks. "Then stay with me. We should be able to decide our fate. If you want to be with me and me with you, I say to hell with everything else. Let's do what we want."

"Is it really that simple?" I clasp my arms around his neck.

He tilts his head down, his lips so achingly close to mine. "We can make it so."

The second our lips touch, it's like a blast of electricity bolts through my body. Every single passion and desire I had for Tate explodes tenfold. My wolf stirs inside of me, and there's only one word that comes to mind. *Mate.* I break away from the kiss, gasping for air.

Tate grips onto my arms, his breaths hard and quick. "Did that just happen?"

When I look into his eyes, it's different. It's like I can see into his soul and feel what he's feeling. The connection we had before is much deeper now. I can feel it coursing through every fiber of my being.

"It's you," I whisper. "After all this time, it's been you all along."

Tate slides his hands down to mine. "At least we know our feelings are real. I fell for you long before tonight."

I rest my head against his chest. "Same."

"Now, all we have to do is wait for the full moon." As soon as he says the words, I gasp and look up at him. I want to bond with him, but that's not the problem. The full moon is still fifteen days away. Our situation just became that much direr. "Faith, what's wrong?"

"You," I murmur sadly.

His gaze narrows. "Me? What do you mean?"

"If word gets out about this, you'll be a target. As long as I'm unmated, I'm still fair game. If Killian and his men find out, they'll hunt you down."

Tate shakes his head. "They won't find us, Faith." He grabs my face and kisses me, my body melting against his. I open up to him and moan as he claims me with his lips. A low growl erupts from his chest as he tastes me. He sucks my bottom lip between his teeth and slowly lets me go. "We don't have to tell anyone what happened tonight. We'll move around until the full moon, and once we complete the bond, we'll be untouchable."

"Will it really be that easy?"

He shrugs. "It's the only choice we have. I say we go back tonight, pack up our things for the next two weeks, and leave. We can go somewhere Killian, and his men won't think to find us."

An idea comes to mind and I smile. "I know the perfect place."

We ran back to the cabin and changed clothes before leaving Yellowstone behind. A part of me wanted to stay, to be alone with Tate for the first time as his mate, but it's not in the cards for us yet. As soon as we got to Tate's house, I gathered up all my bags and set them by the front door. I know where I want to go, but the problem is getting there quickly and unnoticed.

Dawn soon approaches, and the sun shines its warm rays through the windows. Tate's been on the phone for the past hour, and I've stared at mine, knowing I should call Micah.

Taking a deep breath, I press on his name and listen to the line ring. He picks up quickly, and I can hear the concern in his voice. "Hey, you okay?"

"I'm fine," I reply.

"You never call me *this* early."

"I know, I'm sorry. There's something I need you to do for me."

"Of course. What's up?"

He's going to have a ton of questions. "Can you contact Ian Randale and tell him I won't be coming next week? The same goes for Colton Redding."

The line goes silent for a few seconds. "Do you mind telling me why?"

I bite my lip. "I can't. The fewer people know, the better. You have to trust me."

There are another few seconds of silence, but then he chuckles. "He's your mate, isn't he?" It kills me not to say it out loud. I just feel like the second I do, the whole world will know. "It's okay. You don't have to answer me. I'm sure you have your reasons for what you're doing."

"I do," I assure him.

"Then, in that case, I'll make the calls. Do me a favor and stay safe."

"I will. I promise I'm in good hands."

He snorts. "I'm sure you are."

Rolling my eyes, I can't help but laugh. "When this is all over, I'll come home. I can't wait to see everyone again."

"We'll be here."

We say our goodbyes, and just as I put away my phone, Tate walks into the living room with his bags. "Good news. Chase's private jet will be here in an hour to take us to Florida. We'll land in Tampa and drive the rest of the way, just in case word gets around. If someone comes looking for us, they'll have to search the whole state."

"Oh, thank God," I say, breathing a sigh of relief. I was afraid we'd have to drive the whole way there. The Florida Keys is a place I've wanted to visit for a long time. With nowhere to run free as wolves, it's not a popular destination for shifters. Plus, it's on the opposite side of the country. "Did you tell him about us?" I ask.

He shakes his head. "No, but I know he's wondering. He didn't come out and ask me."

"Micah has his assumptions too," I admit. "He said he'd call Ian and Colton to let them know I won't be joining them."

A mischievous smirk spreads across his face as he pulls me into his arms. "Is it bad I'm pleased about that?"

I giggle. "Nope. You got me all to yourself just like you wanted."

His brows lift. "Didn't you want it too?"

Lifting up on my tiptoes, I kiss him. "More than anything."

"Good. You're going to have me for a very long time."

That's what I'm looking forward to. "Did you call your parents?"

He nods. "They know we're leaving and that I'll tell them everything when we get back. I also called Anson and told him to take over for the next couple of weeks."

Everything seems to be coming together. "Awesome. I guess we're ready to go then." The sound of a car draws closer, and I recognize the rumble as Kami's Jeep. "Did you tell your sister?"

His brows furrow. "No. I don't know what she's doing here."

Kami pulls up and grabs the covered bowl from her passenger's seat before getting out. She runs up to the door, and I open it. "Good morning."

She grabs her chest. "Good. You're awake. I had the craziest dream last night. Afterward, I couldn't go back to sleep, so I made you some blueberry muffins." She hands me the bowl and my mouth waters. Tate and I haven't eaten anything since we left Yellowstone. When she walks into the house, she notices Tate standing off to the side. "Good morning, brother."

He chuckles. "Morning." Then to me, he nods toward our bags. "I'm going to load up the truck." He grabs some of the bags and heads outside.

Kami looks around in confusion. "Are you two going somewhere? Please tell me it's to have some fun."

I shrug. "Yes and no." I'm hoping to have fun, but it's mainly to keep him from getting killed.

Tate comes back in and fetches the rest of the bags. As soon as he's gone, Kami glances curiously back and forth at us. "I had a strange dream last night."

"Oh yeah? What was it about?"

Her grin widens. "You and my brother. He was your mate. I saw you two, so clearly it almost seemed real."

Mouth gaping, I stare at her. "That *is* strange. Where were we?"

She closes her eyes. "It reminds me of the lake by my family's cabin. You and Tate played around in the water, and I was on the shore, laughing with someone else. I don't know who was with me, but I know he was *my* mate. I kept trying to see his face, but I couldn't."

Chill bumps run down my arms. "How do you know Tate was my mate in your dream?"

Her eyes open. "There was magic swirling around you. I was the only one who could see it." I'm stunned into silence. Could it be a coincidence, or does she have special magical abilities?

"Have you had these kinds of dreams before?" I ask.

She shakes her head. "Not until you came into town. I've also dreamt about two other wolves in my pack. Wouldn't it be crazy if they end up being mates?"

"It would," I say, staring at her in awe. "Keep me updated if they do."

"I will." She laughs and looks around, clearly oblivious to the notion that she could have magical powers. "So, where are you and Tate going?" When I don't answer, her face grows serious. "Wait, what's going on? Did something happen?" It's as if everything falls into place. Her eyes widen, and she gasps. "Tate's your mate, isn't he? I knew something was different about you two."

I place a hand over her lips. "This is very important, Kami. You can't say anything to anybody. Tate's in danger, and I have to keep him safe. This is serious."

She nods. "You're scaring me, Faith. Should I be worried?"

"I hope not," I say. "We just have to make it to the full moon without anybody finding us."

"I can't believe my dream was real. That's crazy."

"It is," I agree. "If you have more like that, write them down. You may have developed some kind of shifter power no one has ever had before."

Her eyes light up. "Wouldn't that be something?" I look out the window at Tate, and so does Kami. "Are you going to wait until the full moon to be with each other?" My wolf stirs impatiently inside of me. There's no way I can wait two weeks to make love to Tate. I want him now. A smile lights up my face, and she giggles. "Okay, I have my answer. What about the blood sharing?"

The thought of Tate biting me and vice versa so we can open our mental bond excites me. He'll be able to hear my thoughts, and I can do the same with him. "I'm ready for it, Kami. What I love most is that Tate and I told each other how we felt before the signs even appeared. I know what we have is real."

Tate walks into the house and leans against the doorframe. "So much for secrets."

Kami runs over and hugs him. "I won't say a word. Just know I'm happy for you." She winks at me and steps out. "Have fun and be careful."

I stand beside Tate, and he drapes an arm over my shoulder as we watch her leave. "How did she guess?"

"That's the crazy thing. I'll explain it to you later."

"Can't wait to hear this."

I laugh. "It'll blow your mind."

SEVENTEEN

TATE

Faith is mine. Those words have replayed over in my mind the entire plane ride to Florida. There's never a rhyme or reason why things happen when they do with our kind. I'm just glad the signs appeared before she left for Randale's pack. The thought of her going to him or any other wolf pissed me off. Deep down, I guess I always had the feeling she belonged to me. Looking at her, with her blonde hair blowing in the wind and the sun on her face, I know there's no one as beautiful as her in the world.

We landed in Tampa and decided to drive the six-and-a-half-hour distance to Sugarloaf Key where we have a small beach house waiting for us. It's in a private area with its own secluded beach. There will still be other houses close by, so we won't be able to shift without risking the chance of someone seeing us. For the most part, we'll be alone, which is all that matters.

Faith hasn't been able to stop looking out the window since we left the mainland for the Keys. "I have never seen so much water in my life. It's absolutely breathtaking."

Sometimes I forget she hasn't been able to travel the world

and see things like the ocean or tropical islands. I love that I get to experience her firsts with her. "I was five years old the first time I saw the ocean. My parents couldn't get me out of the water."

Faith giggles. "Yeah, I figured you liked being in the water. You tossed me into your pool and tackled me into the lake."

I wink at her. "And when we get to the house, we'll swim in the ocean and watch the sunset."

She grins. "I like that idea."

Reaching over, I grab her hand and bring it to my lips. She welcomes every touch, and I can feel how happy it makes her to be close to me. If only the full moon were tonight. I've always been a patient man, but having to wait two weeks for her to be entirely mine is fucking torture.

We drive across another long bridge from Long Key to Duck Key. Faith stares out the window in awe. "There are so many bridges."

I snort. "Just wait until I drive you across the seven-mile bridge. It's coming up shortly."

Her mouth gapes. "Wow. Seven miles? That's a long bridge."

"It is," I agree. "You're not scared to go across it, are you?"

She sticks her chin out. "I'm not afraid of anything." I love how strong and determined she is. She'll make a great female alpha for our pack. When we get to the seven-mile bridge, Faith takes out her phone to video it. Seeing how excited she is to see the Florida Keys, I can only imagine how she'll feel when I take her all over the world.

Once we arrive at Sugarloaf Key, it doesn't take long to get to the beach house. It's a three-story light blue estate on a secluded stretch of the Atlantic Ocean. I grab our bags out of the trunk while Faith enters the passcode to get the key out of the lockbox. After we walk in, I set the bags on the living room floor, and we tour all of the rooms.

"Which bedroom do you want?" I ask, picking our bags back up.

Faith's eyes twinkle. "Will you be staying in there with me?"

I've been trying not to overwhelm her with my need, but when she says stuff like that it's hard to keep control. "If that's what you want."

She strolls up to me and presses her lips to mine. "It is."

"Then I guess we'll both take the master suite." I carry our bags to the bedroom, and she follows me. "The sun will be set within the hour. Do you want to go for that swim?"

I set our bags down on the bed, and she opens hers up, pulling out a skimpy bikini with a mischievous grin on her face. She knows what she's doing to me. "I do. It won't take me long to get ready."

She reaches for the hem of her shirt and starts to lift, but then my damn phone rings. I reach into my pocket for my phone where Cedric's name is displayed on the screen. "It's Cedric."

Faith smiles. "Go. I'll change and see you out there on the beach."

"Okay," I say, cursing Cedric under my breath as I walk out of the room. "What's up, brother," I answer.

"I should be asking you the same question. What's going on? Micah tells me you and Faith ran away together."

A chuckle escapes my lips. "You make it sound like we eloped." Having a wedding isn't something shifters do. When we bond on the full moon, that's our ceremony.

"Seriously, Grayson. Was there any indication that Killian and his men found you? I think he's moved on from here."

"No. There's been no sign of him."

"Is Faith okay?"

"She's fine," I assure him. "She came here willingly with

me. You know I would never force her to do anything she didn't want to do."

Cedric sighs. "I know. I trust you. I also know we're friends, and you've never kept anything like this from me before. It has me wondering what's truly going on."

I can't help but laugh. "You really are a nosy son of a bitch."

"Well, it got me thinking. Either Faith was in danger, and you had to get out fast, or something else happened. Maybe you didn't want to share her with the other wolves."

"No, I didn't," I admit, my voice darker than I wanted. "I hated the thought."

Cedric chuckles once. "That's all I needed to hear. I think I know now."

"Know what?"

"That she's your mate."

I should've known that out of everyone in my life, Cedric would be the one to figure it out. "Nothing ever gets by you."

"Nope," he laughs. "After Micah called, Laila and I put two and two together. She said it's probably best you did disappear, and you most likely have a price on your head right now."

"That's what Faith said."

"Well, I'm happy for you. Your life will never be the same. When you get back in town, we'll celebrate."

"Sounds good." Faith turns the corner into the living room, dressed in her sexy black bikini. She struts past me to the patio door and smiles as she walks out. "Convel, I gotta go."

We say our goodbyes, and I hurry into the bedroom to change out of my clothes. When I get out onto the beach, Faith is already swimming around in the water.

"The water is so warm." She floats on her back with the mounds of her breasts sticking out of the water. My cock twitches and I groan.

"Where's the stone?" I ask, hoping she has it on her body

somewhere. I swim over to her, and she latches her arms around my neck and her legs around my waist.

Her smile widens when she feels how hard she's made me. "It's in my hand. There was nowhere else to put it."

"As long as you have it on you." There's one question that's been on my mind ever since Faith and I started to get close, but I've never asked her. I circle my arms around her and pull her in tight. "Have you ever been with a man before?"

She bites her lip. "No, but I've been ready for a long time." Her legs grip me harder, and she gently thrusts her hips against me.

My hands slide down to her ass, loving the way her skin feels. "I don't want to rush you."

"You don't have to worry about that. I'm ready for you to claim me."

Hearing those words lights my body up like fire. The need to plunge into her and take her right there is so great I don't even know if I can control myself. Faith's eyes start to glow, and I know mine does the same.

"Faith," I growl.

She digs her fingernails into my back. "Just kiss me."

I kiss her hard, squeezing her ass and moving her up and down my cock. I may not be inside of her, but I know she's close to a release. I can smell how turned on she is, and I fucking love it. Deepening the kiss, I slide my tongue against hers, savoring the taste of her lips. I move down to her neck, nipping her with my teeth, but not hard enough to draw blood. That's what I want, though—her blood. I want to be able to see inside of her head and her into mine. It's a connection so many of our kind dream of. There's also another effect of sharing blood. When true mates drink the other's blood, they get thrust into a vision of their future. It's one way they get to see what awaits them.

"Can I taste you, Faith? I want to be inside of you, to see our future."

I nip the tender spot behind her ear, and she moans. "Yes. I want to taste you too."

Pulling back, I stare into her glowing, heat-filled blue eyes. Every time I touch her, the fire grows between us. "Then do it," I growl, pressing my lips roughly to hers. "Take what you want."

She sinks her teeth into my lip and sucks it greedily. The second she tastes the first drop of my blood, the connection opens in our minds. "Oh, my God," she breathes, tilting her head back. I slide my lips down her neck and sink my teeth into her skin. She tastes like berries and sunshine. I don't know how else to describe it other than euphoric.

The world begins to fade away, and another scene takes place. Faith and I are in bed, making love. It feels as if I'm really there. With her legs spread wide, I'm pushing into her as I suck her nipples. Her screams of enjoyment spur me on even more. She orgasms and holds me tight, just as I release into her. We kiss and then I'm thrown out of the vision with my cock feeling as if it's getting ready to explode.

"Tate?" Faith whispers in my mind.

"I'm here. The link is open." We can now hear each other's thoughts and communicate silently. We can also block the other out if we want.

Breathing hard, I hold onto Faith and she's gasping for air. "Holy shit, that was intense."

"Yes, it was."

She pulls back and stares into my eyes. "It reminds me of the dream I had of us the other night."

This is news to me. "Oh yeah? Just like that?"

"Yes," she murmurs, kissing me gently. "It was a good dream."

"I tell you what. We have a lot going on right now. As

much as I want to carry you inside and make love to you all night, I don't want to rush things with you."

Her smile widens. "Such a gentleman. Okay, I agree. You'll still sleep in the bed with me, right?"

I snort. "You know it. I'm not letting you out of my arms."

"Good," she says. "Then after tonight, I can't promise I'll be able to keep my hands to myself."

I can't promise I'll be able to do the same either.

EIGHTEEN

FAITH

I've always wondered what it'd feel like to find your mate. Hearing stories about it is one thing, but experiencing it is another. I crave Tate's touch like I can't get enough of him. Even holding his hand as we walk down the beach feels fantastic. There's a burning feeling inside my gut that aches for more. Last night, Tate did what he said and held me in his arms all night. It's the best sleep I've had in a long time.

"Happy to help," Tate says in my mind.

I smack his arm. "Nosy, much?"

"Hey, you're the one thinking it."

We can laugh and banter back and forth with each other, which I've always thought would be important when finding a mate. I look over at Tate and smile. I have to believe the goddess of the moon listened to my prayers. Maybe we do get the choice on who our mates are.

Tate meets my gaze and grins back. The sand feels amazing on my feet, and the hot summer weather is perfect. It almost makes me feel as if our troubles are far behind us, but in all reality, we're in more danger than I could ever imagine.

"Not that I don't love spending time with you, but I have a feeling these next two weeks are going to move like molasses," I say.

Tate's grin fades. "Yeah, you're probably right. Would you still agree to complete the bond so quickly if you didn't have others hunting you down?"

"*I would seal the deal tonight if it was the full moon.*" The words play out in my mind before I can even say them.

Tate squeezes my hand and pulls me to him. "That's all I needed to hear." It's going to take some getting used to with him in my head.

He kisses me, and I wrap my arms around his neck. "I'm ready to be yours, Tate. Nothing is going to change that." His cock twitches, and I bite my lip, wishing like hell I could control myself. I'm ready to feel him inside of me like I saw in the vision.

"Should we head back?" Tate asks, trying to hold back a smile. I know he heard what I just thought in my mind.

"Sure," I reply, feeling my cheeks burn.

He squeezes my hand, and we slowly walk down the beach toward the house. The crystal blue water is calm because of the barrier reef, so no waves are crashing against the shore. It's very calming and serene.

"There's something we need to talk about, Faith."

Brows furrowed, I look into his eyes. "What's wrong?"

He shrugs. "Nothing's wrong. It's just we haven't talked about what's going to happen after the full moon."

"What do you mean?"

Sighing, he peers out at the ocean and then back to me. "I don't want to take you away from your family and friends. I know you just got your sister and brother back." He stands in front of me and takes both of my hands in his. "What I want to know is if you'll be happy with my pack."

His concern is endearing, and it's one of the things I admire about him. How did I ever get so lucky? Tears burn my eyes, and my heart swells with more love for him. "By your side is where I belong, Tate. Will I miss my family? Of course, but I'm happy to know I'll soon be a part of your pack." I can feel his relief, and it makes me smile. "Besides, you need me in Montana. Someone has to make that yard of yours look decent."

He tilts his head back and laughs. "Hey, I think it looks pretty amazing right now." It does, but I have to give him hell. "What about your teaching job? You're supposed to start in the Fall."

I was looking forward to the position, but I have to believe there'll be other opportunities in Montana. "It's okay. I can find something else to do."

His grin widens. "I think I have an idea."

"Do tell," I reply.

"What would you say about working for me? Anna said she knows a ton of people who'll pay big money to have you paint for them."

This makes me smile. "I'd be happy to. I want to share my art with the world in any way I can."

He brings my hand up to his lips and kisses it gently. "I know you want to see the world, Faith. I'm going to do everything I can to make sure that happens."

I step closer to him. Yes, traveling the world was the only thing I wanted once I got my freedom, but it's not as important now. "I'm not in a hurry. Having you is all I need."

His eyes flash, and I can feel his desire to claim me. "How did I get so lucky?"

A chuckle escapes my lips. "I asked myself the same question earlier."

After we got back to the house, we drove to the market on Cudjoe Key since it was the closest. Our dinner consisted of grilled chicken, roasted potatoes, and green beans. Tate grilled the chicken while I did the rest. He's determined to catch our dinner one night by reeling in some snapper. He says he catches fish all the time in the lake by his Montana house. Luckily, the place we're renting has a utility room full of heavy-duty fishing rods.

Time started ticking by, and I didn't realize how nervous I was for the night to come. I know what I want. My body yearns for Tate's touch, my wolf is dying to claim him, and my heart is so full I feel as if it's going to explode. My whole life I've had to be strong, to show no weakness. Feeling nervous is not something I'm used to. Tate didn't say a word when I told him I wanted to take a shower. I'm pretty sure he could tell I was tense, but at least, it's in a good way. Standing in the hot running water and listening to it rush down the drain helped clear my mind. I'm ready to give myself to him in every way.

I turn off the water and open the shower door to grab my towel. Closing my eyes, I listen to the sounds around me. Tate's in the bedroom, which is just on the other side of the bathroom door. The TV is on, but I know it's not loud enough to drown out the sound of my rapidly beating heart.

Wrapping the towel around my body, I stop at the door and release my breath. When I open the door, I look at Tate lying on the bed, and all the nervousness disappears. He has one arm behind his head, still dressed in his gray T-shirt and jeans. He turns off the television and looks over at me, his lips parting into a seductive smirk.

"There's no rush, Faith."

"I know," I whisper, letting the towel drop to the floor. His eyes flash as he takes in my bare body, and I know he's holding back the urge to ravish me. "But I'm ready for this." I stalk closer to the bed. "I'm ready for you to make love to me." Those words are all it takes for the fire to consume him. Hell, I can feel the burn too.

In one quick motion, Tate is off the bed and picking me up in his arms. I wrap my legs around his waist, loving the feel of his hardness against me. A low growl escapes his lips as he places me on the bed, his body covering mine.

"I don't want to hurt you."

I look up into his glowing blue eyes. "You're not going to."

He lowers his lips to my neck, up to my cheek, and across my lips. I devour him, tasting him greedily. I don't think I can get enough. Tate's soft, warm lips trail across my breasts, and he sucks my nipple like a ravenous wolf. I arch my back, wanting him to suck harder. My insides tighten and clench with need. He separates my legs with his knee and thrusts his hips against me. The movement alone has me close to orgasm.

"Please, Tate. Make love to me," I say, voice husky and breathless.

Smirking seductively, he takes my bottom lip between his teeth. "I have to make sure you're ready."

Taking his hand, I slide it between my legs so he can feel how wet I am. "I'm way past ready."

A deep, satisfied growl rumbles in his chest. "Yes, you are." He rubs my clit gently before slowly entering me with his long, warm fingers, thrusting them inside of me. I move my hips along with his strokes, and the orgasm builds until there's no way I can stop it from coming.

"Tate," I cry out, closing my eyes as the force of my release has me exploding from the inside out.

WHEN I OPEN MY EYES, Tate's heated gaze is on mine. "You are so fucking sexy."

I grab the waistband of his jeans. "I need more. And I know you do too."

His eyes flash to his wolf's, and his need overcomes me. He slides off the bed and removes his shirt and jeans within seconds. My body trembles at the sight of his naked body. Biting my lip, I spread my legs wide, inviting him in. He climbs on top of me, holding my face in his hands as he gets into position. Without wasting any time, he enters me deeply, and I hold my breath. The sensation of him filling me is euphoric.

"You feel so fucking good," he moans, dropping a hand to my breast. Still rocking his hips against mine, he lowers his lips to my nipple, flicking his tongue against me. He sucks me harder while thrusting deeper inside of me. My release builds to the point I feel like I'm going to scream. I graze my nails down his back as it grows stronger and stronger.

Tate grunts with his thrusts, and it turns me on even more. "I know you're close. I can feel you getting tighter."

"I am." I rock my hips harder against his, and I instantly fall over the edge as my release explodes all around me. Tate grabs my face and kisses me, keeping his hungered gaze on mine as he deepens the kiss and finds his own climax. His cock pulsates inside of me, and I love the way it feels.

Breathing heavily, Tate rests his forehead to mine. "That wasn't a disappointment for your first time, was it?"

My heart races out of control. "Definitely, not. I thoroughly enjoyed it." He slowly pulls out and rests beside me. I lay my head on his chest and smile. "I think I want more."

Tate laughs and rubs a hand down my back. "I'm pretty sure I'll be up for that."

When I look down at his body, he's more than ready for another round. He tilts my chin up and looks deep into my eyes. A few seconds pass, and all we do is stare at each other.

There's so much longing and love in his eyes that if I were standing, I'd be weak in the knees.

"I love you," he murmurs.

Tears burning my eyes, I lift up so I can kiss him and breathe him in. I want to remember this moment for as long as I live. "I love you too."

NINETEEN

FAITH
TWO DAYS LATER

Paradise can only describe what I've been in the past couple of days. Each day, Tate and I have explored several of the different islands of the Florida Keys that are close by. My favorite is Big Pine Key with its secluded Bahia Honda State Park. We snorkeled for hours, and I held onto my stone the entire time to make sure I was protected. I found some exquisite seashells that I know Bailey and my friends will love.

Today, however, Tate and I decided to take it easy. He's determined to catch our dinner for tonight, and I'm having fun watching him do it all while drinking a berry cider we picked up in Key West. It makes the perfect drink for a day out on the beach.

Tate casts his line out into the water and glances at me over his shoulder. *"You sure do look sexy laying on that towel,"* he says through our bond.

I smile. *"Maybe you should join me. No one's around."*

Even though he's a little way down the beach, I can still hear him chuckle. *"Dinner time will be here before we know it. I can't give up just yet."*

"Okay. I'll just admire you from afar." His shorts ride low on his hips, and his bare chest glistens with sweat. There are only ten days left until the full moon, and I'm counting them down.

A few minutes pass and my phone begins to ring. I haven't been getting many phone calls since Tate and I arrived in Florida, only because we thought it best to go incognito. If Killian knows the right people, he could easily have them tap into my phone line and figure out where I'm at. I look around for my cell, and it's under my tank top. Kami's name is on the screen when I pick it up.

"Hey. Is everything okay?"

"I know I'm not supposed to call, but I have to tell you this." Her voice sounds frantic.

My heart rate must've alerted Tate because he turns to look at me. When he sees that I'm on the phone, he rushes over. "What happened?" I ask Kami.

She blows out a breath. "Okay, so remember me telling you about my dreams?"

"The one about Tate and me?"

"Yep, and the one about the other two wolves. Their names are Nina and Flynn. It just so happens that they're mates. The signs showed up last night. Word spread through the pack like wildfire this morning."

Tate kneels down in the sand, watching me curiously. "Oh, my God," I reply. "That's amazing. I'm putting you on speaker so that Tate can hear."

"What all does it mean, Faith? It could be a freaky coincidence or ..."

"Or it could be something big," I finish. "Shifters with magical abilities are special."

Tate sighs. "They also become targets."

I nod in agreement. "That's true." I look down at the

phone. "What made you dream of Nina and Flynn? Did you interact with one of them recently?"

She gasps. "I did. Holy shit, I didn't even think about that. I ran into Nina at the sandwich shop during my lunch break. That night was when I had the dream."

"There has to be a connection to that somehow. You were also around me, and you dreamt about Tate and me. Whatever you do, keep this to yourself, Kami. I don't know what it means or why it's happening to you." It truly is fascinating, and I can't wait to see what comes of it. "Honestly, I think it's pretty interesting that you can see future mates together in your dreams."

She snorts. "I see mine too, but not his face. It's weird having him in my dreams and touching him, but not being able to see who he is."

Tate chuckles. "Yeah, that is kind of strange."

Rolling my eyes, I shake my head. "Strange and kind of awesome. I wonder if you'll ever get a clear view of him."

"I don't know," Kami says. "Only my dreams will tell." She blows out a breath. "Okay, I'll let you two go. I just thought I'd call and let you know."

"Keep me updated if you have more dreams," I tell her. "When everything settles down, and I can safely come back, we'll figure it all out."

"Perfect. I'm ready to have you both home."

Home. It brings a smile to my face to know that my home is with Tate. We say our goodbyes to Kami, and I lay back on the towel. Tate sits to my side and looks down at me. "If what she has is a gift, don't you think we might need to keep it a secret altogether?"

I shrug. "Maybe. If people like Killian knew, they could exploit it." She'll have wolves coming in from all over the place, seeking her out to help them find their mates. That could turn into a disaster really quick and fast.

Tate growls low. "I'll kill anyone who goes after my sister."

"So will I," I promise him. "When we go back to your pack, I'll train Kami and all the females who want to learn how to fight."

Tate's shoulders relax. "That would absolutely make me feel better. I want them as strong as you."

I wink. "They will be."

He opens the small cooler beside my towel and looks in to find it empty. "What happened to all the ciders?"

A snicker escapes my lips. "I got thirsty watching you fish."

Getting to his feet, he picks up the cooler and laughs. "I'm going in for more. Do you need anything from the kitchen?"

I shake my head. "I'm good."

He takes the cooler and walks toward the house while I lay back and rest my head on the towel. The sand is soft underneath, making the perfect pillow. Closing my eyes, I listen to the sounds around me. Seagulls squawk in the sky, and I can hear the current of the water. On mine and Tate's next adventure, I want to go somewhere with waves.

My body starts to get heavy, and I can feel myself drifting off to sleep. It feels good to give in.

Opening my eyes, I bolt up when I see the sun about to set in the distance. I grab my phone and look at the time, seeing that I've been asleep for almost two hours. How is that even possible? Tate is nowhere to be seen.

"*Tate?*"

I try to concentrate on our link, but all I get is silence. The hair on the back of my neck stands on end. Something's not right. There's nothing but quiet all around me, even from the house. Tate's heartbeat is all I hear, and it's slow, very slow. The only reason it'd be that way is if he's sleeping and there's no way in hell he would've left me outside alone while he took a nap. Grabbing my phone, I click on Micah's name. There's nothing he or my pack can do, but I can at least alert them if something were to happen to me.

Me: I think we're in trouble out here.

His reply is instant.

Micah: Where are you?!?!? Run if you have to.

Me: Not running. Sugarloaf Key, Florida.

He's going to be pissed at my reply, but I can't leave Tate. I refuse to. Killian and his men have done this before. The eeriness surrounding me feels familiar, just like the night he came for me. Grabbing my tank top and shorts, I slip them on quickly, making sure the black carmine stone is in my pocket. Anger wells up in my chest, and I stalk toward the house. If he or anyone else hurts Tate, I'll rip them limb from limb and not think twice about it.

When I get to the back porch, the glass sliding door is open like it's taunting me to enter. *"Tate? Please answer me."* Still, nothing. I walk inside, and that's when I see him on his stomach, out cold on the kitchen floor. From what I can see, there's no one else in the house. Unfortunately, it doesn't mean they're not there.

Rushing over to Tate, I kneel and push him onto his back. "Tate, wake up," I demand, tapping his cheek. He doesn't budge. "Dammit! Wake up!" Clenching my teeth, I stand and jerk around, knowing I'm not alone. "Come out, asshole. I know you're here."

A chuckle echoes down the hallway. Killian. He turns the corner, grinning mischievously. "It's good to see you again, Faith."

"I can't exactly say the same," I snap. "How did you find us?"

He shrugs. "It wasn't easy." He flourishes a hand up and down my body. "There's some kind of magic at play here. I'm assuming your good friend, Laila, did that."

"It's a black carmine stone." The sound of the sultry voice makes me freeze. It has to be Tia, his witch. She strolls into the living room, dressed in a long, black dress with her chocolate-colored hair pulled up in a ball of curls. Her sea-green eyes stare down at my shorts. "It's in her pocket."

I try to think of a way to get out of there with Tate, but Killian is by one exit, and Tia stops by the back door. I have no doubt it was her magic that made me fall asleep earlier. She could easily put me out again.

"Did you have a good nap?" Tia asks, her lips spread into a smirk.

"Go to hell," I hiss. Then I turn my glare to Killian. "It's sad you have to use magic to take us out."

He chuckles. "I'll do anything to get what I want. Would you rather I killed your friend instead? It could've been easily done." A growl echoes from my chest, and he holds up a hand. "I'm not here to fight you, Faith. No one is going to hurt Tate Grayson. He'll wake up when we're long gone from here. If he wants to see you again, he'll get the chance."

It's obvious they don't realize he's my mate. I need to keep it that way. His words, however, confuse me. What reason would he have to let Tate see me again? "What are you planning?"

Killian steps closer, his eyes raking down my body. "You'll find out soon enough. Right now, we need to get on the road. We have a long journey ahead of us. You can either play nice or ..."

My first instinct is to fight, to rip off Tia's head and put an end to it all. The only problem is that she'd put me to sleep before I could even wrap my hands around her neck. "Fine," I growl, holding my hands in the air. "I'll come without a fight."

Tia laughs. "Oh, Faith, you expect us to believe that?" I don't want to be put down, but I can sense her magic drawing closer. My eyes grow heavy, and I feel myself falling, but

Killian picks me up in his arms. I can't move or speak, but I can still hear them. "We can't have her trying to rip your throat out on the plane," Tia says. Plane? Where the hell are we going?

Killian chuckles, and his nose grazes my neck as he breathes me in. "True. I think that'll change once everything's said and done." Once what is said and done? I want to hear more, but the darkness seeps into my body, dragging me under. *Tate* ...

TWENTY

My eyes shoot open, and I'm on the floor. Growling, I get to my feet, my wolf desperate to break free. Fucking Killian. I'm going to kill him if it's the last thing I do.

"Faith, can you hear me?" Closing my eyes, I concentrate on our link, but it's silent, just like it was when I tried to get her to run away. Tia had put a spell on her to make her sleep so she wouldn't hear us in the house.

My body shakes with rage as I replay it over in my head.

Reaching into the refrigerator, I grab a few more beers and put them in the cooler. Before I can close it, my arms and legs begin to feel heavy. "What the hell?"

"Look who I found?"

I jerk around, but it takes a monumental effort, like a colossal weight presses down on me. The second I get a good look at the cocksucker in front of me, it doesn't take a genius to figure out who he is. Killian Vilkas. He even has his fucking witch beside him.

"How the hell did you find us?" I hiss. I try to reach Faith

through our bond, to tell her to run away, but it's like I've been blocked.

Tia waves her hand in the air, and I drop to my knees. She saunters over to me and traces a long, red fingernail across my cheek. "Wolves are so sexy when they're pissed."

Gritting my teeth, I glare up at her. "You won't be saying that when I'm ripping off your head."

She leans in close, and I fall to the floor, fighting to stay awake. "You're a strong one."

Killian chuckles. "But not strong enough."

My wolf fights to break free, but he's trapped. The weight presses down on me, crushing me to the floor. Killian walks over to the back door and looks out, grinning when I know his eyes fall on Faith. He peers over at me and winks. "Sweet dreams."

The darkness creeps over me, and I try to fight against it, but Tia's voice echoes in my ear. "Nu sunt dușmanul tău." I have no clue what it means, but I know not to forget it.

My phone buzzes in my pocket, pulling me back to reality. It's Micah, but I'm not ready to speak to him. The last thing I want to do is tell Faith's pack that I failed. When I look at the time, four fucking hours have passed since Killian took her. I run outside, and the only trace of Faith is the towel she laid on. I hurry back inside, and all of her belongings are gone in the bedroom.

Scrambling around the room, I throw all my stuff together in my bag and call Faith's phone. It has to be somewhere in the house. The call goes through, but I don't hear it ring anywhere. But then a voice answers on the other end.

"I figured you'd call at some point."

"Where the fuck are you taking her, Vilkas?" I demand.

He laughs. "Don't worry, she's fine. She's just sleeping it off for a while. We're about to take off. I'll be more than happy to tell you how to find her. You just have to be willing to pay the price."

"What sick game are you playing at?"

"No game," he laughs. "Are you in or out?"

"In," I growl. "Now, where are you taking her?"

"I have to get there first, Grayson. I'll call you when it's time." And with those words, he hangs up. Fucking bastard. I scroll through my contacts and press send on Chase's number. I need his jet to get me back to Montana ... and fast.

It's early morning, and I'm almost home. The jet ride felt like an eternity. I spent the entire time wondering where Faith was and if she's truly okay. I hate myself for what happened. I talked to Micah and found out that Faith had sent him a text to alert him that something was wrong. He and some of the others from Faith's pack had a head start and are on their way to my house. They should be there when I arrive, along with my family and Anson, if I can ever get in touch with him.

When I pull up to my house, the driveway is full of cars. Kami rushes out and races over to me. "Where's Anson?" I ask her. "I haven't been able to get in touch with him."

She throws her arms up in the air. "Hell, if I know. Everyone has been trying to call him. No one around here has seen him either. Ansley was on her way to his house not long ago, so hopefully, she'll get some answers." Ansley is Anson's sister and one of Kami's close friends.

Red flags shoot up in my head. "How long has it been since anyone's seen him?" I haven't spoken to him since I left for Florida.

She follows alongside me up to the house. "Ansley's the last one. It was the day you left." I pause mid-step and look at her. She blows out a sigh, her gaze concerned. "Dad tried calling him about a job the other day too, but he never got in touch with him."

"Why didn't you tell me?" I ask her.

She shrugs. "We didn't want to worry you."

"I don't have a good feeling about this." He's the only one who knew how to find Faith and me.

"Neither do I," she admits.

Where the hell could he be? My dad comes out on the front porch with Micah, Colin, Cedric, and Laila. Micah walks forward and slaps a hand to my shoulder. He can see the turmoil on my face. "Nobody blames you, Grayson. It happened to me too, and I'm her protector."

Colin agrees with a nod. "It could've happened to any of us."

Nothing they say is going to help. I failed at protecting Faith, and I'll have to live with that for the rest of my life. "Yeah, but I'm her mate," I say. Colin's eyes widen, and my dad gasps. Micah, Kami, and Cedric already guessed it earlier. I'm pretty sure Laila knows because of Cedric.

My dad places his hands on my shoulders. "Oh, son. I'm so sorry."

"We have to find her, Dad. I won't rest until I do."

He nods. "You will. And when you do, you'll bring her home, and we'll make her a part of the family."

I want to know she's okay. As long as Killian and his witch don't find out Faith and I are linked, we'll be safe. I'll be able to connect with her when she wakes up.

"Come on," I say to everyone, "there's a lot you all don't know." They follow me inside and gather around my living room. I can feel my patience running thin. All I want is to find Faith.

"Is there anyone who knew where you were?" Micah asks.

I nod. "Anson, my second-in-command. It turns out he's missing." I have my thoughts about what could've happened, and none of them are good.

My dad steps forward. "Do you think he turned on us?"

"No," I say in all seriousness. "He would never do that. If Vilkas and his witch traced Faith to here, they could've used magic to infiltrate his mind somehow. It's the only way they would've gotten the information out of him. He would die before betraying me."

"So, what do we do now?" Colin demands. "We can't just sit here. My sister's out there."

"We're not," I growl. "I'm going to find her. Killian's an alpha. He'll feel the strongest on his own turf. That's why I think he's probably headed to Canada."

"I agree," Laila cuts in. "I know him."

"Let's head up there now," Colin states adamantly.

Cedric places a hand on my shoulder. "Did you by any chance share blood yet?"

Everyone looks at me, and I nod. "We did. But right now, she's under Tia's sleeping spell. I can't get through to her. When she wakes up, we'll be able to communicate. If they knew I was her mate, they would've killed me."

Colin throws his hands up in the air. "What the hell is this Vilkas fuck doing anyway?"

Clenching my teeth, I run a hand angrily through my hair. "I don't know yet, but when I called Faith's phone after I woke up, he answered."

Gasps erupt in the room, but Micah's the one who speaks up. "What did he say?"

I look around at everyone. "He said that if I want to see her again, I'll have to pay the price. He'll call when he gets to his destination."

The room falls silent. I'm more than ready to head up to Canada if that's where she is. It's a gamble no matter what I do since there are so many unanswered questions and uncertainties. Not knowing is driving me in-fucking-sane. All I want is to talk to her, to make sure she's okay.

Loud, thunderous knocks sound on the door, and my dad

hurries over to open it. Anson's twin sister, Ansley, rushes in, her breathing frantic. She looks just like him only she has green eyes whereas his are gray. Kami runs over to her. "Oh, my God, what's wrong?"

"Have you heard from your brother?" I ask her.

She turns to me and bursts out crying. "Anson was taken, Tate. I don't know who they are."

Kami pulls her into her arms when she starts to hyperventilate. "Ansley, it's okay. Breathe. Tell us everything."

Eyes wide, I step toward her. It takes her a few minutes to get settled down. She wipes away her tears but more flow. "I went over to his house to check on him, and the door was unlocked. He never leaves his house unlocked when he's not there." She sniffles. "I went inside and looked around but couldn't find anything amiss. That's why I decided to check his camera footage."

A sinking feeling settles in my gut. I don't know what I'm about to hear, but I know it's not good. "What did you see?"

Her lips tremble. "Two people. A man and a woman." As soon as she says that, I already know it was Killian and his witch. "They knock on the door, and when Anson answers, words are exchanged, and when he tries to go on the attack, he falls to the ground." She closes her eyes and sobs. "The guy tossed him into the backseat of the car, and they drove away."

"Motherfucker," I growl. "That's how Killian found out."

"Does Anson know anything else important?" Micah asks, intentionally not saying what that is in front of Ansley.

I shake my head. "No, he doesn't know."

Kami leads Ansley to the door. "It's okay, Ans. We'll find your brother and bring him home." Ansley nods, and she walks her out.

"What the fuck?" Colin shouts. "How is this Vilkas bastard figuring all of this shit out?"

Laila steps in. "Magic. He wouldn't be able to otherwise. Tia comes from a long line of Romanian witches."

"How many are like her in the world?" I ask.

She shrugs. "Not many."

My father places a hand on my shoulder. "What are you going to do, son?"

I look into his blue eyes, which are the same color as mine. "I'm going after her. No one's going to take Faith away from me."

Colin and Micah both stand next to my father, and Micah says, "We're going with you too."

TWENTY-ONE

TATE

It's been settled. Colin and Micah are both going with me. It turns out that Faith's pack is good friends with an FBI agent who graciously looked up Killian Vilkas and sent me everything about him. There wasn't much, but I did get his address. We all grabbed the money we needed from our banks and headed on our way to the airport where Chase's jet will take us where we need to go. By the time everything's done, I'll owe him my life.

Before leaving Montana, I asked my dad to watch over the pack. There's no other person I trust. With Anson gone, I have an even bigger problem with Killian. He took my mate and my second-in-command. The man's going to die for it.

I didn't realize I was clutching the steering wheel so tight until my fingers started to go numb. I look over at Micah, and he sighs. "I get it. I'm tense too."

He's probably wondering the same thing I am. How the hell are we going to get Faith out of Killian's compound without Tia using her magic on us. And compound is the right word. I looked at the aerial view of his property, and it's gated.

Colin's phone beeps for the hundredth time, and he

moans. "Don't get me wrong, I love my sisters, and I'd do anything for them, but they can be pains in the asses."

He's typing away on his phone when I glance at him in the rearview mirror. "Is it Bailey again?"

His eyes meet mine through the mirror. "Yep. She's asking if you're able to get through to her yet."

I shake my head. "There's nothing. It's different from when she's sleeping. That's how I know she's under magic."

Colin focuses back on his phone. "All right, I'll let her know." We arrive at the small, private airfield, and Chase's jet is there waiting for us. "It's nice having friends with their own planes."

We get out of the truck and grab our bags from the back. "Yes, it is. I know he's disappointed your sister didn't turn out to be his mate."

Colin slings his bag over his shoulder. "I'm sure a lot of people will be pissed when they find out she's taken."

I was happy when Cedric found Laila but also envious. Some wolves wait decades to find their mates. After what happened between Faith and me, I'm starting to think it's not as complicated as it appears. I think we do have the choice, and it'll happen when you're ready.

We all walk toward the jet where the pilot, James, is there waiting for us. "With all the royal females claimed, that leaves two," I say to them. "You're both royal arctics. I've seen how the women in my pack act around you guys."

Colin snorts. "Faith said we should go around visiting to see if our mates are part of the other packs like she did with you and Maheegan. If she only knew how volatile men like us are, especially if an outsider comes into our territory."

Even though I love the fact that Faith is trying to help our people, he has a point. When unmated males feel the rage, it's hard to keep a level head. If there's someone not part of the pack sniffing around, it triggers the anger. Granted, I've never had to put any in my pack down, but I've heard of it happening to others.

We get close to James, and he smiles. Faith and I had talked to him a lot on the way to Florida. He's human and closing in on sixty-years-old with white hair and an average-sized build. His wife passed away two years ago from cancer, so he's devoted all of his time to being Chase's private chauffeur. He said it would give his wife joy to know he's out exploring the world.

"It's good to see you again, James," I say, shaking his hand.

He smiles at us all. "Same to you, Mr. Grayson. And to you," he says to Colin as he shakes his hand. Then he turns to Micah. "I think you're the only one I haven't met."

Micah holds out his hand. "I'm Micah Lyall."

James shakes his hand. "James Campbell, nice to meet you." He nods up at the jet. "I believe we're ready to go when you are."

I nod. "Sounds good."

He grins. "Great. I'll be in there waiting."

Once he's in the jet and out of earshot, Colin and Micah focus on me. "What if she's not in Canada?" Micah asks.

She could be anywhere in the fucking world right now. That's what kills me more than anything. I feel like a fish in shallow water, gasping for air. Desperate. "Let's hope she is," I reply. I'm trusting my gut.

TWENTY-TWO

FAITH

"*Faith, can you hear me? Faith.*"

His voice echoes in my mind, and when I open my eyes, I almost expect to see him. "*Tate?*" The relief I feel is almost overwhelming, but then reality sets in.

"*Thank fucking God. You're awake. Are you okay?*" he asks, his voice pained.

Sitting up, it takes a few seconds for my eyes to clear, and when they do, I see I'm not alone. "*I'm fine, but I'm not alone. Tia's here in whatever room I'm in. I have no clue where I'm at. Are you okay?*" Everything comes flooding back. Florida. Killian. Seeing Tate unresponsive on the floor in the kitchen.

"*I'm fine. Your brother and Micah are with me.*"

Sitting across the room at the window seat and reading a book is Tia. She looks over at me and smiles as she shuts her book and walks toward me. Wearing a yellow sundress with her chocolate-colored hair in loose waves down her back makes her appear less like a seductress than in the black gown she wore the last time I saw her. I know not to be fooled by her, though.

"I'm sorry I had to keep you under for so long. I wanted to make sure everything was perfect."

"Perfect?" I scoff. "How can things be perfect? You kidnapped me."

"Tate, can you see and hear everything?"

"Yes," he answers. *"I'm right there with you. Make sure to focus on her so she doesn't pick up on anything."*

Tia's smile fades. "Kidnap is such a strong word. This isn't a prison, Faith. You're not going to be locked in here." She waves her hands about the room. "I think it's quite a lovely room. I had it prepared for you."

The walls are a light green with white, gossamer curtains to go with the white, lacy bedspread that covers me. It all seems so light and airy, not like the darkness I know surrounds me. Tia strolls over to one of the doors and opens it to reveal a closet where some of my clothes hang neatly.

"Your dresses and nice clothes are in here," she says. Then she nods over at the antique white dresser on the other side of the room. "And your T-shirts and underthings are in the drawers."

I look down at my clothes, and I'm still wearing the same tank top and shorts over my bathing suit. "How long have I been out?"

"Two days."

My head jerks up. "Seriously?" If I was out for two days, that means there are only eight days left before the full moon. "How did you find me?"

I expect a smart-ass response, but all she does is shrug. "Magic has its perks, I guess."

"They have Anson, Faith. It's how they were able to figure it out."

Averting my gaze, I slide off the bed. *"Is he okay?"*

"I don't know."

I walk past Tia to the window and peer out. There isn't

anything around except for vast land and a river in the distance—no other buildings or houses. There's just a road that leads in and out through the gate that's attached to a tall, brick wall expanding as far as I can see.

"Where are we?"

Tia comes up behind me. "Canada. Killian's estate."

Tate's audible sigh can be heard in my head. *"I'm not far from you, Faith."*

I turn around to face Tia. "What did you do with Tate? Did you just leave him on that kitchen floor?"

"He's okay," she says, her voice sounding tired. "I'm pretty sure he'll be headed this way soon."

My heart rate spikes. "Why is that?"

All she does is stare at me, but then she shrugs. "I just have a feeling."

"Why am I here?"

There's a sadness in her eyes, but then her demeanor completely changes when the sound of footsteps thump down the hallway. "I'm going to let Killian explain all of that. He's giving you time to take a shower and get changed."

"Oh wow," I retort sarcastically. "How nice of him."

Tia smiles once and nods. "All right, I'll leave you to it. The book I'm reading is fascinating. I left it on the window seat for you."

I stare at her blandly. "Gee, thanks."

Turning on her heel, she walks out and quietly shuts the door. I wait to hear a locking sound, but nothing happens. When I twist the knob and open the door, I peek out, and the hallway is vacant.

"They have to be tricking me somehow. They're not just going to leave the doors unlocked."

"That's because the witch can simply use her magic," Tate counters.

I close the door and sit back on the bed. *"What happens*

now? I don't know what to do." He feels so close to me being in my mind, but that couldn't be further from the truth. I'm so afraid I'll never see him again.

"You're going to see me again, Faith. I can promise you that."

I can't help but smile. *"You're listening to my thoughts. I guess I need to hide them better."*

"I like hearing your thoughts. I've been without them for two days, and it fucking killed me. I didn't know what was going on."

Lying back on the bed, I close my eyes. *"I was terrified when I saw you on the kitchen floor. If we were mated, Tia's magic wouldn't work on us. We'd be stronger than anything she could throw at us."* When two wolves mate, their bond can withstand just about anything. It makes them almost indestructible. That's why so many wolves want to find their mates.

"I know," Tate murmurs. *"We'll get there. When Killian found us in Florida, he told me I could see you again if I pay the price. He said he'd call when it's time."*

"And you have no idea what he means by that?" I ask.

"No. Hopefully, he'll tell you tonight."

The thought of having to be around him makes me livid.

"It pisses me off too," Tate growls, *"and he better keep his fucking hands to himself."*

"Don't worry about me. I know how to rip those hands off."

"Keep calm, Faith. As much as I'd like for you to do that, Killian holds all the cards right now. If you fight against him, all he has to do is get Tia to spell you and you're out. I need you awake."

Groaning, I open my eyes and sit up. *"Fine. I'll play nice for now."* If I'm to meet Killian for dinner, I need to get mentally prepared.

"I'm not leaving you, Faith. I love you."

I wish I could hold him and feel his arms around me. *"I love you too."*

AFTER TAKING A SHOWER, I put my wet hair in a braid and dressed in a pair of jeans and one of my looser T-shirts. The last thing I want is to look sexy. I even opted for no makeup.

"You still look sexy as hell. Every man who has eyes will see that."

I move to the door and place my hand on the knob. *"I'm trying to look dull and unappealing."*

"Just be careful, Faith. And stay strong. Micah told me how your anger gets the best of you sometimes."

I open the door and peer out. No one is in the hallway. *"I'm trying. Tell Micah I won't lose my focus. I know what's at stake here."* My life.

"Good."

If I didn't have Tate in my mind, this would be a lot harder. He gives me the strength I need. Taking a deep breath, I move out into the hallway. There are paintings on the walls, all elegant and beautiful, but I can't bring myself to enjoy them. On one end, the hallway stops, and there's a large window that overlooks the land. The other end of the hallway leads to a fancy staircase that goes down. I slowly walk to the stairs, expecting to see movement on the lower level, but it's quiet. It has to be a test to see if I'll run because even though it's quiet, I can feel Tia's magic all over the place. There are wolves around; but I can't sense them yet.

I take the white marble stairs down the spiral staircase and stop when I get to the bottom. The house is enormous, with its open foyer and an expensive chandelier hanging from the ceiling. I can either go out the front door or choose one of the four hallways.

"There you are." I look to my right, and Killian is there, grinning as he rakes his gaze over my body. Dressed in a pair of jeans and a dark blue T-shirt, he looks the same as before with his light brown hair and bright green eyes. "Want to take a walk with me? I'll show you the house."

"I can't wait to kill that bastard," Tate growls in my mind.

"Sure," I reply.

Killian flourishes a hand down the hallway he just came from. "We can start here."

We walk down the hall, and he shows me all the various bedrooms and bathrooms. When we get to the other side of the house, there's a library, a study, and a media room. I don't care about any of it, but I nod and try to show interest. It's all so grand and over the top. My family is worth a lot, but I have no desire to show it off like that.

When we get back to the foyer, I look around curiously. "If you don't mind my asking, where does all your money come from? You don't deal drugs, do you?"

He bursts out laughing. "Hell no. It's time you learned the truth as to why you're here. I don't see the need in keeping it from you, especially not when the fun's about to start."

The way he says it makes shivers run down my spine. I'm not sure what his idea of fun is, but I doubt it's anything but that. He opens the door, and I follow him outside. The tall, brick wall I saw from the window expands around his property, locking us in. "Fun, huh? Why am I not getting that vibe?"

He glances back at me and smirks. "Lighten up, my little wolf. You'll be thanking me once this is all over." I highly doubt that. It takes all I have to bite my tongue.

We walk around the side of the house, and I still haven't seen anyone else. There's a pool in his backyard and gardens all around. "Where's your pack? I'm surprised you don't have me locked up."

. . .

"THAT'S NOT what I want, Faith. I want you to be comfortable here. I told you before you'd be treated like royalty, and that's what I'm trying to do."

He takes me around the gardens, and we head through the field to the giant workshop building at the edge of his property. "What is that place?" The closer we get, the more my gut clenches with uncertainty.

Reaching into his pocket, he pulls out what looks to be a garage door opener and presses the button. The massive door to the building opens, and I hold my breath, wondering what I'm going to see on the other side. When everything comes into view, it's not what I expected at all. The walls are full of built-in shelves filled with various tools and piles of wood. And in the middle of the room are two giant drafting desks and table saws.

"Woodworking?" I ask.

Killian runs a hand over one of the desks. "Yep. It's my hobby." He grins at me as if there's a joke in there I'm not understanding.

Gaze narrowed, I stare at him. "So, if woodworking is just a hobby, what do you do for real?"

His eyes flash, and I can feel his excitement. "Follow me."

We exit through a door that leads us further into the workshop. The hallway is narrow, and when we turn the corner, there's another door. Killian opens it, and there's a stairway that leads into darkness. The hair on the back of my neck stands on end. I can smell blood and death mixed with wolfsbane, even if it is faint and covered up by the scent of bleach.

"What the hell is down there?" I growl.

Killian chuckles. "You're not afraid, are you?"

"No, but I'm not stupid. I don't know what you do in your basement of Hell, but I know it's not something I want to see."

"It's all for you, Faith."

If blood and death are all for me, I don't want anything of it.

"You can do this," Tate assures me. *"I have to know what he's planning."*

Inside, I groan. Why me?

With a heavy sigh, I wave for Killian to continue. "Go. I need to see this." I dread getting to the bottom of the stairs. The walls are solid concrete, and it's dark and cold.

Killian turns the corner first and flips on the light switch. I step off the last stair and peek my head around the corner. My mouth gapes when I see the underground world Killian had made for himself. When I think of the building above us, the basement is three times larger. It had to have taken years for Killian to construct something like this. Unfortunately, I now know where the blood and death come from. There are three fighting rings, surrounded by cages and barbed wire at the top. Hundreds of stadium chairs circle all three. Visions of people cheering on others as they fight to the death in the ring flash through my mind, but I push it out.

"Oh, my God." I can feel Tate in my mind, but his silence makes me nervous. He most likely thinks what I'm afraid to think.

Killian flings his arms out wide, proud of his masterpiece. "This is how I make my money."

Mouth gaping, I circle around, taking it all in. "How's that?"

He cuts a glance my way. "Seriously, Faith? You don't know?"

Clenching my teeth, I huff. "You make money off fights. I've heard about this stuff with humans, but not our kind."

His grin widens. "That's the beauty of it. Human fights are boring. Our people know how to make it gritty and exciting."

I throw my hands in the air. "What the hell are they fighting for?"

Killian shrugs. "Money. Power." He pauses for a second. "A mate."

"Motherfucker," Tate thunders in my head. *"So that's what he's doing."*

I didn't want to think it, but I was afraid it would lead to that. "How can you fight for a mate?" I snap. "The magic of the moon doesn't work like that."

Killian shrugs again and steps toward me, his face more serious than I've ever seen him. "Maybe, maybe not. It's not only unmated males who yearn for a mate, Faith. You may not believe this, but it was the women in my pack who agreed to this arrangement many years ago when my father was alpha. It made them happy to be mated off to men who'd fight and die for them. I continued the tradition for a while, but when word got out about the royals, suddenly normal female wolves weren't good enough." Stunned into silence, I was not expecting to hear that the females came up with the idea. Guess it's not far-fetched to believe it. Women have needs just as strong as men. "All I know is that your pack members are being matched with the strongest of our kind. Take for example, your sister and Ryker. He defeated the Yukon pack, and now he's more powerful because he's a royal's mate. Their kids will have the royal bloodline. The same thing goes for Tyla and Sebastian and your good friends Laila and Cedric."

My mouth gapes. "How do you know all of this?"

He throws his arms in the air. "Everyone knows. Why do you think I got you out when I did? If I didn't take you, someone else would have, and I bet they wouldn't have been as nice as me. I could've easily killed your royal protector and your friend, Grayson, but I didn't. At least, you're safe now, and the men who wanted to come after you can fight for their chance." His smile comes back. "Speaking of which, I told your buddy he could see you again if he was willing to pay the price. Do you think he'd come here and fight for you?"

"You better fucking believe it," Tate hisses.

"I don't know," I reply. "Why don't you call him right now and find out?"

Killian's eyes twinkle. "Oh, I plan on it. I think he'll make a great fighter. Plus, he wants you just like all the other men."

Anger fuels through my veins as I slide past him to stand next to one of the fighting rings. There are bloodstains on the white mat and fur caught in the barbed wire. I don't want to imagine Tate inside the cage fighting against another wolf. "So how will this go exactly? You make bets on the fighters, and then whoever wins gets me?" I turn and glare at him.

He gives me a devilish grin. "Oh, no, my little wolf. The men are paying to fight for you. Only the strongest will win. You deserve the best."

"The best?" I shout, storming over to him. "What if the winner's a complete and utter asshat? I'm not mating with anyone against my will. Your plan is absolutely fucked up beyond belief."

"It won't be like that. I promise."

I push past him and head toward the exit. *"Calm down, Faith. I'm just as pissed about this as you, but you have to play along somehow,"* Tate warns.

I stop mid-step and close my eyes. How in the hell can I play along with this? But then, an idea comes to mind. I face Killian again and stare right into his flashing green eyes. He doesn't even conceal his need for me. "How do you know it won't be like that?" I ask. "You can't control who wins this fight."

He stalks toward me. "No, but you can. I'll let you figure out how you want to do that." He stops only a breath away from me and peers down into my eyes. "I need you to trust me, Faith. I'm not here to hurt you in any way. It'll be a win-win."

"Something tells me this fight will be rigged from the begin-ning," I say to Tate.

I can feel his rage. *"You're right. We just have to figure out a way to beat him. I wonder if he's competing himself."*

"Okay, I'm in," I huff, staring back up at Killian. "When do the fights start?"

"Tomorrow. My men will be meeting the contestants at a secure spot at Baker's Ridge and bringing them here."

He's too close, so I step back and walk to the stairs. When I get there, I glance at him over my shoulder. "What's in this for you?"

His heat-filled gaze bores into mine. "The chance for a mate. I'm competing too." Now I know for sure it's rigged. He would never allow anyone to come into his turf and beat him. He nods toward the exit. "You're free to roam around the grounds and go wherever you like. I'll discuss more of the details at dinner."

Heart racing, and not in a good way, I take the stairs one at a time, wondering what the hell I just got myself into.

TWENTY-THREE

TATE

The bond between mates works in mysterious ways. If I concentrate hard enough, I can almost see through Faith's eyes. I can hear what she hears and see what she sees. Having that privilege can also be detrimental. Controlling myself when my mate is around another unmated wolf who wants her doesn't make things easy. I warned Faith about controlling her temper, but I made it more difficult for her. She can feel my rage, just like I could feel hers.

We just landed at the Baker's Ridge airfield. There isn't much in this part of Canada. You can only get to the area by plane. I can see why the Blue River pack can stay hidden and how no others can sneak and attack them. If I succeed in getting Faith away from Killian, it'll be challenging getting out of Baker's Ridge. It's something we'll have to deal with when the time comes. I don't want Faith knowing my concerns, so I intentionally block her from those thoughts. She needs to focus on keeping her head in the game.

Colin peers out one of the airplane windows where you can see the small town several hundred yards away. We could probably walk the entire span in thirty minutes. "There's only one hotel here?"

I grab my bag and sling it over my shoulder. I've already told him and Micah everything that's going on, but I'm still waiting on that call from Vilkas. "Yep. Along with one bank, one grocery store, one gas station, and so on. There were only two rooms left at the hotel when I called. I'd imagine they're pretty booked up with all the shifters in town." I reserved both of them, one for James and the other for the rest of us.

Micah stands and picks up his bag. "I wonder how many are competing."

The thought infuriates the hell out of me. Faith is mine. "I don't know, but I'm sure it's a fuck ton." Faith has been quiet since she walked away from Killian and his underground fighting dungeon. There are times when she blocks me out just like I do with her, but I don't say anything. We both know what we're up against. My guilt eats away at me for not being able to protect her.

James opens the door to the cockpit. "Isn't this an interesting place," he jokes.

I snort. "You have no idea."

He opens the jet door, and we take the steps down. I can sense shifters all around us in the town. I look up at James. "You have a room at the Baker's Ridge Hotel. I put it under your name."

James nods. "I'll check in once I'm done here."

"Sounds good," I say. "I'll keep in touch. When the time comes, we might have to get out of here pretty quick and fast."

I don't know what Chase has told James, but he never asks any questions. "Don't worry, I'll be ready," he replies. He disappears back into the jet while Colin, Micah, and I walk through the airport property to the exit.

"Do you think he'll be okay on his own out here?" Micah asks. "This place is overrun with shifters."

"It won't be for long." If what I suspect is going to happen, most of them will be dead soon.

When we get out of the airport gate, the town is just a few steps away. It consists of six streets, the three main ones being businesses and the other three are full of small houses.

"Have you heard anything more?" Micah asks.

I shake my head. "Faith's keeping her emotions from me right now. She's alone walking through the gardens."

Micah sighs. "That's where she likes to be."

"She's supposed to eat dinner with that cocksucker tonight, so I'm sure we'll get more information then."

Colin grumbles. "I can't even imagine what it's like for you right now. She's my sister, and I'm pissed off as hell. If this were my mate, I'd be murderous."

I'm trying to keep my anger from Faith, but it gets harder the longer I'm away from her. "Trust me, I am."

By the time we turn the corner to one of the busy streets, that's when several shifters come into view. There are a couple here and there, going in and out of the buildings. However, when the three of us get noticed, the level of hostility in the air thickens.

It's not hard to figure out why. "They know you're both royals," I say to Colin and Micah.

Colin projects his power out like I knew he would. He likes the attention, whereas Micah keeps it more lowkey, just like me. "Good," Colin growls. "They need to be afraid."

Micah scoffs. "These men don't seem afraid at all. If anything, you're adding more fuel to the fire. Knock it down, Storm."

Colin huffs. "You're no fun."

"And you're being irresponsible," Micah counters. "We need these people to underestimate us."

Royals can conceal their strength, so Colin obliges by

toning down his power. What they don't know is that I can do the same thing.

"They'll be surprised when you unleash it," Faith murmurs in my head.

I smile. It feels good to have that connection with her. *"I like being underestimated. It'll be a good fighting strategy."*

"I should know more at dinner. Right now, I'm enjoying being alone. Although, I have the feeling I'm being watched."

"Of course, you are. Vilkas isn't going to leave his grand prize unattended."

Micah bumps me with his shoulder. "What's Faith saying? I can tell you're talking to her."

I huff. "She's saying how she'll get more information at dinner."

"It'd be nice if Vilkas would call," Colin grumbles. "I'm ready to know what the fuck's going on." That makes two of us. I can't afford to be hotheaded like him, not with Faith's future and my life at stake.

We come upon the small hotel, and once inside, the place is a little rundown with its worn-out lobby furniture and dusty smell. There are two shifters at the bar who glare at us, but then they go right back to their drinking. The young lady at the desk is human and must be no more than twenty-five years old. She grins wide as we approach, especially when she locks eyes with Colin. "Good afternoon, gentleman. Are you here to check-in?"

"We are," I say, drawing her attention to me. "It should be under Grayson."

She clicks away on the old computer. "Is there a bachelor party or something going on? We've never been sold out like this. I've had over two dozen young men check-in today."

If she only knew. "Something like that," I reply.

She turns and grabs a set of keys off the wall. "All right, I got you on the third floor, second door on the right."

I take the keys. "Thanks."

We take the stairs, which creak with every single step until we get to the third floor. I don't expect much when I slide the key in and open the door, but it's surprisingly not as bad as I thought. The room is clean, and there are two queen beds. I toss my bag onto one of the beds and look out the window. There's one long road that leads out of town toward the mountains. Killian lives out that way. If he doesn't call, I'll have no choice but to figure out a way to get her out.

"His property is surrounded by a brick wall and guarded by people at the gate, Tate. I don't see how you could get in without getting yourself killed," Faith says.

"Listening in on my thoughts?"

Her sigh sounds sad in my head. *"Under normal circumstances, I wouldn't, but it gives me comfort to listen to you."*

"Same with you," I reply.

My phone rings, and I pull it out of my pocket to see a number I don't recognize. "Is it him?" Micah asks.

Turning around, I look at him and Colin. "Don't know, but we're about to find out." I press the speaker button. "This is Tate," I answer.

"Ah, Grayson, it's so good to hear your voice."

I nod at the others, so they know it's him. "Vilkas. I can't exactly say the same for you."

Killian bursts out laughing. "Now, now, I told you I would call. But if you don't want to see Faith again, I can let you go."

I growl. "You know I do, asshole. What do I have to do?"

"For starters, you need to fly to Baker's Ridge, Canada, and arrive by tomorrow morning. Think you can do that?"

"I'm already here." The line goes silent, and I smile. "Yeah, that's right, cocksucker. You're not the only one who can find people."

"I'm intrigued," Killian replies. What I love is that I can hear the uncertainty in his voice. "Are you alone?"

"Does it matter?" I snap.

"It does. There's only room for one more fighter. You see, the wolf who wins the grand finale gets the prize. From what I know about Faith and her pack, I can assume either her protector or brother came with you."

"And if they did?"

Killian chuckles. "You'll have to figure out amongst yourselves who's going to compete. If Colin's with you, I'm sure it would make Faith happy to have her brother with her during the fights. The last thing I want is to keep her family away from her."

Colin's eyes widen, but he stays quiet. I don't like this game Killian's playing. "Does Faith know this is going on?" I ask him.

"She knows some of it. I'm going to explain the rest to her at dinner. Is it safe to say I can tell her that her brother will be here tomorrow?"

"Yes," Colin growls.

"And me too," Micah cuts in. "Not unless you're scared to have her protector with her."

Killian laughs again. "Well, hell, this is unexpected. You're more than welcome to come, Micah. I can't wait to give Faith the good news." All I can think of is that it's a trap. "All right, here's the deal," he continues, "my men will pick you up at the abandoned shack at the edge of town tomorrow morning at ten. It's two hundred and fifty thousand to fight. Hope you brought your money, Grayson."

"Oh, I'm prepared."

"Good. You fight at noon. You'll all see Faith when you get here."

"What about Anson? Where is he?" I demand.

"You'll see him soon." He hangs up, and that's it. I'll never forgive myself if something happens to him because of me.

I slide my phone back into my pocket. We all look at each

other, and Colin is the one who speaks. "Do you really think he'll let me stay with Faith?"

The way Killian says Faith's name with such familiarity enrages me. I know what game he's playing at, and it's not going to work. "I think he will," I say in all seriousness.

His brows furrow. "How's that?"

I turn back to the window, desperate for the morning to arrive. "First off, he has a witch who can put even a royal into a sleeping coma. And second, it's obvious what he's trying to do with allowing you and Micah to spend time with Faith."

Micah blows out a sigh. "I see it now. He wants to get in Faith's good graces. That way, he doesn't seem like the villain. It gives him a chance to get close to her."

I can feel Faith in my mind. *"This is interesting. I might have to test out this theory."*

"Don't do anything stupid, Faith. Killian's an unmated male and one who wants you. You can only go so far."

"I know. You have to trust me. I know what I'm doing."

I surely hope so.

TWENTY-FOUR

FAITH

I spent the entire afternoon walking around Killian's property, discreetly trying to find a way out, but there are cameras everywhere. The wall is too high to jump over, and if you did manage to get to the top, some lasers would set off an alarm. I wouldn't get too far.

There's a bench in the garden surrounded by butterfly bushes, so I walk over to it and sit down. It's times like these where I wish I were something other than a shifter. If I was fae, I could transport myself with my magic and be somewhere else.

Closing my eyes, I tilt my head back and breathe in the crisp, cool air. It's summer, but it doesn't get hot in north-eastern Canada as it does in the states.

"Good evening."

My eyes snap open, and I gasp. "What the ..." I hadn't heard a single footstep draw near. It confirms my suspicion that Tia has her magic concealing everything. There's no telling how many people are on the grounds watching me.

The man is a shifter and dressed in a suit with an earpiece latched to his ear. He reminds me of someone you'd see in a mafia movie. Then again, that's how it is with some alphas. You have packs who live in the mountains so they can run free, and you have some who are right in the big cities, using their shifter strength to take charge. It's been way too long since I've been able to shift. I don't see how the big city shifters can deal with the trash and nasty smells of city life.

The man in the suit holds up his hands. "Didn't mean to scare you, Ms. Storm. My name's Marcus. Mr. Vilkas is waiting for you on the terrace where dinner will be served shortly."

I get to my feet. "Thanks." The terrace is on the other side of the house.

Marcus flourishes a hand in the direction I need to go. "If you go that way and turn to the right, you'll see the terrace."

"Okay. I'll go right now." He nods once and walks in the opposite direction.

"Very fancy," Tate grumbles. *"Vilkas has way too much fucking money."*

I start down the path. *"That's because he and his family used the women in their pack as cash cows. It benefited them all, I guess. Maybe that's why some of the men in Laila's old pack never came back after Killian visited them. They went off to fight for a mate and didn't survive."*

"That's probably true."

Turning the corner, I see the terrace up ahead with a table set for dinner. Killian stands when he sees me and smiles.

"Here we go," I say to Tate. *"Hopefully, he'll tell me more. What he said to you was vague. You fight tomorrow at noon, but against who? What does it entail? This is what I need to know."*

"I'm right there with you."

As I draw closer, Killian pulls out my seat for me. "How was your afternoon?"

"Quiet," I say, sitting down. My stomach growls because I

can smell the food underneath the covered dish. Then again, I don't think I've eaten in two days. "I did a lot of walking."

He sits across from me, and my stomach growls again. "I think you're hungry."

I scoff. "I wonder why? Someone kept me asleep for two days." My first instinct is to refuse to eat.

Tate huffs in my mind. *"You need to keep up your strength, Faith. Just eat the damn food. This isn't a time to be stubborn."*

"Fine." I take off the top of the covered dish. Underneath is a rare steak, baked potato, and asparagus. Grabbing my fork and knife, I dig in, which makes Killian smile even more.

"Have you thought about anything?" he asks.

I stab my fork into the steak. "Oh, you mean about how tomorrow there's going to be God knows how many wolves here fighting to be my mate?"

With a heavy sigh, he glances down at his plate. "Yes, that."

"You know, I'm not one to judge, but if that's what the women in your pack wanted, then so be it. I'm happy they got their mates in the end, but you overstepped when you took me. I never would've agreed to find my mate like this."

He lifts his gaze to mine. "And I told you earlier that you can dictate the outcome of this. Not all of the wolves fighting for you are douchebags, Faith. If the ones that make it through to the final rounds are not to your liking, we'll figure out a way to get them out."

"Isn't that cheating?" I say.

He shakes his head. "Not if it's fair. It just so happens that I got in touch with your friend, Grayson, today."

"And?"

Killian shrugs. "And he'll be here tomorrow with your brother and your protector, Micah."

Eyes wide, I gasp, pretending to be shocked. "What does this mean?"

Killian cuts a bite of his steak and uses his teeth to slide the meat off his fork into his mouth slowly. "It means," he says, chewing his steak and swallowing it, "that you're going to have your family here with you tomorrow. I figured you could be with me when we meet them at the gate in the morning. They can stay as long as you want."

This is where I want to test the boundaries. "Does that mean they can stay here in this house? Like they don't have to leave when they get here tomorrow?"

Killian nods. "Of course."

My heart about jumps out of my chest. "All three of them?"

His eyes flash, and he narrows them. "Not Grayson. He's competing for you. I'll have a war on my hands if the others found out. Your brother and Micah are more than welcome to stay in the rooms across the hall from you, but Grayson has to go back to Baker's Ridge and wait it out like the others."

"Take it, Faith," Tate yells in my mind. *"As long as they're with you, I know you'll be protected."*

"Tia can still use her magic on them," I counter.

"Doesn't matter. They want to be there."

I stare at Killian, wondering what reason he could have for allowing them to stay close to me. "Thank you," I say, gauging his reaction. Is he genuine? Or does he have an evil plan cooking up in his mind? Knowing who he is, I can only think the latter.

He smiles. "You're welcome. Your family and friends are welcome here. I don't want to keep them from you. That's why I'm giving this back." He slides my phone over to me. "Feel free to call them whenever you like."

Taking my phone, I look it over. "What's the catch? Did you bug it so you can listen in?"

He holds a hand over his heart and laughs. "You wound

me, Faith. I'm trying to earn your trust, and you're not giving me a chance."

"It's going to take a lot more than this to earn my trust," I say, staring at him blandly.

"Then tell me what I can do."

I sit back in my chair. "Be honest with me. If you're competing to be my mate, I deserve nothing but that."

"I agree. I'll do anything. I'm trying to show you I'm not as bad as you think by letting your brother and Micah stay here. With both of them together, they're a lot stronger than me."

I snort. "But you have Tia who can knock them out with a flick of her wrist. If you want me to trust you, the way to do that is to make amends with my family and me. You took me away from them. Right now, they're pretty angry."

"Okay," he murmurs, regarding me earnestly. "I won't use magic on them. Does that make you happy?"

"Yes. And you can't use it on me either."

He nods in agreement. Do I believe him? No.

"What else?" he asks.

Focusing on my plate, I cut up my steak. "Tell me about the fights. I want to know everything from the beginning to the end. How many men are competing? Are they fighting to the death? Will they be in wolf form or human? How are you going to keep order with so many shifters here?"

Killian chuckles. "Slow down. That's a ton of questions. I see you've been giving this a lot of thought."

"Just a little," I snap back sarcastically.

"I'm hoping one day you'll be able to talk to me without all the hostility."

This makes me laugh and not in a humorous way. "Seriously? You took away my choices, Killian. How can I not be angry over that? I've been in hiding my entire life. All I want is to travel the world and experience new things. I want to find my mate the *natural* way, to have someone love me because of who I am and not what I can make them. The wolves you have fighting for me just want my royal blood, that's it. They don't know me."

He sighs. "That's why I'm giving you the chance to know them."

I'm about to eat some of my food and freeze. "What do you mean?"

"That's what I'd like to fucking know," Tate grumbles in my mind.

Killian holds up a hand. "I'll get to that. Let me start from the beginning and answer all your questions." He takes a bite of his food and leans back in his chair. "Forty-eight men are competing, all alphas of their packs and from all over the world. There will be twenty-four fights tomorrow, twelve early afternoon, and twelve tomorrow night."

That's a lot of fights and a lot of bloodshed. "What is my role during all of this? Do I have to watch them all?"

Killian shakes his head. "No, but I figured you'd want to see the men and what they're like. You know what you're looking for. As far as fighting to the death, that depends on the wolf. If they back down, they lose and go home, and their opponent advances."

"Are you getting all of this, Tate?"

"Yeah. I've seen some of the wolves. Something tells me they'll all be fighting to the death."

The thought sickens me to the core; so many senseless deaths and for what? My stomach churns, and I push my food away. "Why does that bother you?" Killian asks, genuinely confused. "It's their choice. I'm not forcing any of them to do what they're doing."

I shrug. "Honestly, it's sad. All of those wolves have mates out there somewhere." He looks away, and I study him, wondering what's going through his head. "Just like you," I finish.

His eyes blaze when he focuses back on me. "I've waited a long time to find my mate, Faith." He takes a deep breath and averts his gaze again. I can feel the rage building inside of him, and my wolf is screaming for me to run. The darkness surrounding him sends warning signs all through my body, but it disappears just as quickly as it started. Out of the corner of my eye, I see Tia by the window. Her eyes meet mine, and she stares at me for a second before walking away. With the way she looked at me, it wasn't malicious. It's almost as if she's trying to help *me*, not him.

"What the hell is going on?" Tate demands.

"I think Tia's using magic on Killian. I'm starting to wonder what's really going on in his head. Whatever it is, I don't like it."

"Tread carefully, Faith. Don't provoke him."

It takes a few minutes for my heart to stop pounding. Killian focuses back on his food as if he didn't just about lose his shit.

"How old are you?" I ask, softening my voice. Once we get into adulthood, we look the same for hundreds of years. The only way I've been able to tell the difference is in mannerisms. Killian seems to be a lot older than the thirty-year-old-looking man in front of me.

Killian smiles and lifts those bright green eyes to mine. It's almost as if he's a different person. "A little over a hundred. Why do you ask?"

I shrug. "Just curious. You speak like you're older."

He chuckles. "I'll take that as a compliment."

Even though I'm not hungry anymore, I slide my plate back in front of me and eat a few bites of my steak. "So, finish telling me about the fights," I say. "Will the men be in human or wolf form?"

Killian finishes up his food and sits back. "Both. Fighter's choice. Once the first twenty-four fights are done, the next day there will be twelve to narrow it down even more. After that, we'll have the main events, consisting of three fights for two nights, resulting in six winners overall. The prize for these winners is alone time with you."

"What!" Tate shouts in my mind. *"Fuck no."*

The blood boils in my veins, and I can feel the heat rushing through my body. My wolf wants to tear out of my body and rip everything apart. "What kind of *alone* time are we talking about here? I don't mind going for a stroll or talking, but if these wolves have something else in mind, I'll rip them apart starting with their balls."

Killian's eyes flash to his wolf's. "I'll kill them myself if they try something like that." He takes a deep breath, and his eyes go back to normal. "You'll be safe, Faith. I promise. And with your last question about keeping order, I got it covered. Tia will be on standby in case things get out of hand, and you will have your brother and protector by your side."

I want them here with me, but I'm so afraid it'll be a trap. Killian's unhinged and barely hanging on without Tia's magic, so there's no telling what he'll do. I pick up my phone and scroll through all of my recent calls. There's a bunch of them from my sister.

Killian slides his chair back and stands. "I'll give you some privacy to call your family and friends. You should probably let them know you're okay."

Am I okay? Far from it.

"Thanks," I say, scrolling to Bailey's name. "My sister has got to be worried sick."

Killian disappears inside, and I press the call button. Bailey answers on the first ring. "Faith, is that you?"

It feels good to hear her voice. "Yes, it's me. I'm okay."

She bursts out crying. "Oh, thank God. What's going on? Are you free?"

"No, not free. Far from it. Let's just say I'm neck-deep in some serious shit right now."

"What are you going to do?"

I try to think of ways to escape, but nothing comes to mind. The only way to fight Tia's magic is with magic, and I don't have any of it. "I don't know," I murmur, closing my eyes against the burn. "I honestly don't know."

TWENTY-FIVE

FAITH

After I spent an hour on the phone with Bailey, I called Micah and Colin to let them know they'll be staying with me at Killian's house. They already knew, but I had to assume Killian could hear me. I have to be careful in what I say. For the rest of the night, I laid in bed and talked to Tate the entire time. It made my time alone in the dark bedroom seem less lonely.

"We're getting ready to head to the meeting spot. I'll see you soon, love."

My lips pull back. *"See you then."*

Looking out the window, I watch a van come through the gate, no doubt bringing in other fighters. I saw three others come in earlier. Tia's book sits on the window seat cushion, but I've yet to open it. It looks like a historical romance, but it's in another language. How the hell does she expect me to read it if I don't know what it says. I open the book, and there's a slip of paper inside with writing on it.

Nu sunt duşmanul tău.

I say the words out loud, and Tate comes back. *"What did you just say?"*

"There's a note in this book Tia left me that says Nu sunt duşmanul tău. I have no clue what it means."

"Faith listen, Tia said the same thing to me the night they took you."

Grabbing my phone off the bed, I type in the words exactly as they're written on the note. The translation that comes back to me makes me gasp. *"It's Romanian. It says I'm not your enemy."*

Does it mean Tia's not our enemy? If so, she's making it hard to believe that.

"I don't know, Faith. I wouldn't trust her just yet."

I slide my phone into my pocket. *"I don't. Tia's supposed to be here soon to walk me down to the gate."* Just as I say it, a soft knock sounds on the door. I walk over and open it.

Tia stands on the other side and looks up and down my body, smiling. "You look different today. Guess you're happy you get to see your brother and protector." She looks different as well, more like a vixen in a sexy red dress and red heels. It's much different from her innocent appearance yesterday.

"I am." I stand out of the way so she can enter. Instead of jeans and a baggy T-shirt like I wore yesterday, I decided to put on a pair of black leggings and a stretchy pink top so I can move fast in and rip off in case I need to shift. I want to be prepared for anything.

Tia strolls in, and I shut the door behind us. When she turns to me, I hold up the book. "This is some good reading."

Her eyes dart to the door, and she holds a finger over her lips. "That it is. I thought you might like it." With her finger still over her lips, she holds up a hand, and I close my eyes. It's very faint, but I can hear footsteps down the hall moving further away. A few seconds later, she blows out a sigh. "Okay, we're good now."

Keeping my voice low, I hold up the note she wrote.

"What the hell is this? You expect me to believe you're not my enemy?"

"I'm not. I'm trying to help you as much as I can."

Last night at dinner comes to mind, but I don't mention it. I want to hear what she has to say. "How have you helped me?" I ask, clenching my teeth with anger.

Her eyes sadden, and I can feel her despair, but she snaps right back at me. "You know very well I helped you last night. If I don't take away Killian's rage, he'd have murdered everyone in Baker's Ridge by now. I'd hate to see what he'd do to you. That's why he ordered me to use my magic to lessen the urges."

Shivers run up and down my spine. I don't want to know how Killian would be without her helping him. "So, he's losing his mind to the rage?"

She nods. "Killian thinks you are his only hope."

I shake my head. "I'm not, Tia. You know this. He will never be my mate. You can't force the magic on someone, especially after what you both did to get me here."

"I know," she whispers. Crossing her arms over her chest, she walks over to the window and peers out. "I tried telling him it was wrong, but he wouldn't listen."

"Then why help him? He couldn't have done it without you."

She sighs. "That's what I hate most."

The whole thing is infuriating. "Can't you think for yourself?" I hiss.

Her shoulders sag, and she turns to me, her expression full of turmoil. "I can, and I do. I know taking you was wrong. It killed me to do it, but I literally had no choice. Whatever Killian wants, I have to give him." She huffs and looks back out the window. "My family's been linked to the Vilkas line for centuries. And when I say linked, I mean we're physically linked. It's a curse. That's why I refuse to have children. I don't want to take the risk of having a daughter and her being a prisoner for the rest of her life."

I can't even imagine what that would be like. "So ... if Killian asked you to put a sleeping spell on me right now, you'd have to do it?"

She blows out a sigh. "Yes. I won't be able to stop. Things used to not be this way. Honestly, it wasn't bad being a part of the Blue River pack. Killian's always been nice and respectful to me. I've been given everything I could ever want. I mean, the only thing I hated about his family were the fights, and even those were consensual."

"Can the link be broken?"

Silence fills the room. I walk over to her, and she looks at me. "The only way it can be broken is if I die." She swallows hard. "Or if Killian dies. But that's not going to happen, not while I'm alive."

"How is that?" The look of regret on her face overwhelms me with dread.

"Do I have to spell it out for you, Faith? He told me that if he were to be attacked, I'm to use my magic to hinder them. Why do you think he took you down so easily that night in your cabin?" Mouth gaping, I stare at her in shock. I felt so weak after, like all my training meant nothing if I couldn't defend myself. What if I am stronger than Killian? I'll never know as long as Tia uses her magic to keep him safe. "With that being said," Tia continues, "We both know what the outcome of these fights will be. Killian will win."

Bile rises up the back of my throat. If Tate fights against him, he'll lose. "Oh, God."

Her attention jerks to the door, and she gasps. "I have some ideas, but we can't discuss them now. Pretend all is well."

A couple of seconds later, a hard knock pounds on the door, and it opens. Orin stands on the other side and smiles.

"Well, well, look who we have here. It's good to see you again, princess."

"Yeah, I bet," I grumble.

Chuckling, he moves out of the doorway. "The van will be arriving in a few minutes. I was told you wanted to be at the gate when your friends arrive."

Excitement soars through my veins, but then Tia's warning brings me right back to reality. *"We'll figure something out, Faith. I won't let Killian win,"* Tate murmurs in my head.

You always see movies and read books about good triumphing over evil, but it doesn't work like that. Not in my world.

TWENTY-SIX

TATE

I t's time to meet Killian's men at the abandoned shack. Over the past couple of hours, we watched shifters walk to the abandoned shack and get picked up in vans. Now it's our turn. Micah and Colin have their bags with them so they can stay with Faith at Killian's house. I would rather them be with her.

"You gonna be okay without us?" Colin asks teasingly, trying to lighten the mood.

I sling the bag of money over my shoulders. "Yeah, if I don't get killed."

Micah stares at me with concern. "What are we going to do about the whole Tia situation? We all know you're going to be the one fighting against Killian in the end. She'll have no choice but to use her magic on you."

There's only one way it won't work on me, and that's to seal the bond with Faith. Unfortunately, our circumstance prevents that from happening. The final fight will be the night of the full moon.

In the distance, I can see a black van approach. "Here we go."

The van stops at us, and two shifters get out. The driver says the other guy's name, which happens to be Roman, and I recognize him from Faith's memories. He was the third wolf that came into her cabin that night with Killian and Orin. He opens up the van door and flourishes a hand inside.

"All right, boys, load up. The boss is waiting for you." Micah and Colin get in first, but Roman steps in front of me, blocking my entry. "You got the money?"

He smiles, and I shove my bag of money into his chest, almost knocking him off his feet. "Here you go."

A low growl erupts from his chest. "Get in."

I hop in the back, and he slams the van door closed. A few seconds later, we're on our way. I look at both Colin and Micah. "Whatever happens, keep Faith safe." They both nod, and I can feel the tension mounting. I'm more than ready to do what I have to do. If that means killing every man I step into the ring with, I'll do it without hesitation.

The road north is desolate with nothing but land and mountains in the distance. It takes about ten minutes of flying down the road to get to Killian's property. We come to a stop at the gate, and it slowly opens. I can feel Faith's presence nearby.

"I'm just inside the gate waiting for you," Faith says.

It feels like it's been a fucking eternity since I've seen her. "She's there," I say to the others.

We're driven inside the gate, and I can hear it close behind us. Roman and the other guy get out, and the side van door opens. That's when I see her standing in between Vilkas and his witch. Her eyes lock on mine, and her smile is the most beautiful thing I've ever seen. Colin and Micah get out first, and she runs to them, throwing her arms around their shoulders.

"I'm so glad you're here." She looks at me over Micah's shoulder, and when I get out of the van, she slowly comes to me. Everyone watches us, and I know we have to be careful. Her eyes mist over with tears, and she hugs me. "It's so good to see you."

I wrap my arms around her waist and breathe her in. "Yes, it is."

"I love you." Her words echo in my mind.

"I love you too."

She lets me go and stands back with Colin and Micah. Killian places a hand on both of their shoulders as if they're good friends. Faith gives them a warning glare to play it cool, which they do.

Killian looks over at his witch. "Tia, why don't you show our guests to their rooms?" He smiles at both Colin and Micah. "You'll be right across the hall from Faith."

Tia nods at him. "Will do."

He removes his hands from their shoulders, and they all follow Tia toward the house. Faith sneaks a glance back at me. *"Stay safe, Tate. I'll see you soon."*

"See you soon."

Killian focuses on his two men and waves them off. "Go. I'll take Grayson."

His men leave, and Killian nods for me to walk with him. "Glad you could make it."

"I would do anything for Faith," I reply.

Killian glances over at me and narrows his gaze. "So would I." My insides boil with rage. He took what didn't belong to him as if he had the right. He leads us in the direction of the large building at the edge of his property. Through Faith's mind, I've already seen what it's like inside. We walk through the woodshop and down into the basement, where twenty-three other contenders warm up in their areas. I was the last to arrive.

Killian points at the men stationed around the room. "I have my men standing guard to make sure everyone keeps the peace. This is the first round of fighters. The other twenty-four will fight tonight."

"You must be making a killing off of this," I grumble, not impressed in the least.

He bursts out laughing. "Yeah, a little. That is if I make it to through to the end. I'll be fighting in the group tonight." I have no doubt he'll make it through. "But you'll be happy to know that Faith will get some of the proceeds when this is over."

"He didn't tell me that," Faith informs me. *"I don't want blood money."*

Killian waves a hand throughout the room. "Take a look around, Grayson. Half of these men will be dead in a few hours. Hopefully, you won't be one of them."

"I won't," I say in all seriousness.

He looks at me and smiles. "I like you, Grayson. You're different from the others here."

I glare at him. "How so?"

His grin broadens. "You have heart. You don't see Faith as a prize to be won."

I face him head on. "That's because she's not."

The tension in the room rises, and he steps toward me. "No, she's not. She's mine."

My wolf threatens to break free, but then Faith's voice calms me down. My claws dig into my palms, drawing blood. *"Tate, don't."*

Clenching my teeth, I back up, which is something I've never done. Killian chuckles and pats my shoulder as he walks past. "Good luck, Grayson. Sorry to cut this short, but I have guests to attend to."

As soon as he's gone, I retract my claws and watch the gashes heal within seconds. I hate the thought of him being alone around Faith.

"Hey, listen up," a voice shouts from the center of the

room. I look over, and it's Roman. He waves for everyone to move closer. "The fights will start shortly, but I wanted to go over a couple of things with you first. One, when you get in the ring, anything goes. You will not be allowed to leave the cage until one of you submits, or you're dead. Two, you will not know who you're fighting until it's your turn. Until then, you sit and wait. The royal is here, and you'll be able to see her shortly."

The energy in the room spikes, and it fuels their desire. If I had my way, I'd kill them all.

TWENTY-SEVEN

FAITH

Tate's anger was palpable. I heard what Killian said to him. It's the first time he's claimed me like that. I don't like it, and it pisses me off, but I have to pretend I never heard it.

"Everything okay?" Micah asks.

Tia is across the hall showing Colin to his room. "I'll tell you later," I say, leaning in close to him.

Colin and Tia come into my room, and she smiles at Micah. "You sure you're okay with your room?"

He nods. "I am. Thanks." She gave him the room next to me while Colin has the one across the hall.

Tia clears her throat and gives me a warning glare with her eyes darting toward the door. Someone's coming. A couple of seconds later, Killian appears in the doorway. "I'm so sorry it took so long." He holds out a hand to Colin. "It's a pleasure to meet you." Colin glares at him but ends up shaking his hand. Micah does the same. Killian stands back and smiles as he looks at them. "It's not every day you're in the presence of three royals."

Colin stands close to me. "The pleasantries are nice and

all, but I think it's time we get down to business. What exactly are your plans for my sister? I'm not going to sit by and watch her get mated off to just anybody."

Killian's eyes widen, clearly impressed. "No, I would hope not. I wouldn't expect anything less from her brother and protector."

Micah steps forward. "And what if *you* win, Vilkas? Does that mean Faith will be a prisoner here in Canada? Thousands of miles away from her friends and family."

The room falls silent, and I hold my breath. I wasn't expecting him to say all of that. Killian sighs, and his eyes meet mine. "You won't be a prisoner here, Faith. If I were to be your mate, I'd go anywhere you wanted. We could travel around the world and live in Wyoming if that's what your heart desires."

"The bastard sure is laying it on thick," Tate growls in my head.

Killian clears his throat and focuses back on Colin and Micah. "I don't want there to be hostility between us. That's why I'm trying to make amends. Maybe after the fights this afternoon, we can all have dinner together before the other round tonight? Some ladies in my pack really want to meet you."

And there it is ... another agenda. If one of the women in his pack were to become a mate to a royal, it'd strengthen his clan. Neither Colin nor Micah answers, so I do it for them. "They would be happy to meet them," I say.

Killian chuckles. "Excellent." One of his men comes to the door and whispers something in his ear. Killian nods and smiles at us. "It's almost time, so I'm going to head down. Tia will escort you." Turning on his heel, he disappears down the hallway.

Colin glares down at me. "What the hell, Faith? I don't want to party it up here. I'm trying to figure out a way to get the fuck out."

"Good luck with that," Tia explains. "I have no doubt you can escape. Getting out of Baker's Ridge will be the problem."

Micah scoffs at her. "Why should we even trust you?"

Tia brings a finger up to her lips and lowers her voice. "Faith's not the only one who wants freedom. I have a plan, but we can't discuss it right now." One of Killian's men walks down the hall past my room. Tia waves toward the door. "It's time to go."

Colin and Micah flank me, and we follow Tia out of the room. It's time like these that I wish I could speak to Colin and Micah in their minds as I can do with Tate. His mind is focused on the fight, and I don't want to interfere with that. He needs to concentrate. Everyone is silent as we walk through the gardens and the field to the workshop. If you look at the building, you'd never suspect there was a whole underground world beneath it.

When we get inside, you can't hear anything going on until Tia open's the heavy, steel door that leads down. My stomach clenches, and I take a deep breath. I dread the thought of having to watch Tate fight. Tia takes the first step down, and Colin follows in behind her, leaving Micah to my back.

"I'm right behind you, Faith," Micah says.

Tia walks into the underground room first, and when Colin is seen, everything goes silent. When I turn the corner, my breath is taken away. There are so many shifters, their need hitting me like a ton of bricks. But out of all of them in the room, my eyes find the only one who matters. He's in a corner, shirtless with only a pair of gym shorts on, stretching his well-toned muscles. Tate glances over at me and smiles.

"Glad to hear you only have eyes for me."

Micah nudges me in the back, and I tear my gaze away from him to follow Tia to the seats around the center ring where there are five chairs reserved. Everywhere I go, I feel eyes on me. What I hate more than anything is that many of those eyes will be closed forever once the afternoon's up. We take our seats, and the row behind us is full of women eagerly waiting for my brother and Micah. I want them to find their mates, but not here with the Blue River pack females.

Tia sits beside Colin, leaving only one empty seat to her right. Killian makes his rounds around the room and comes over to sit next to her. Eyes lit with excitement, he says, "Here we go."

It takes all I have not to search for Tate in the crowd. A wolf I recognize from the night Killian and Orin broke into my cabin, climbs up into the center ring, and taps the microphone. While listening in on Tate, I found out his name is Roman.

"All right. It's time to get the tournament started." He points to the ring at his right. "Over here, I need Mitch Grayland and Parks Redkin." The room turns electric as both fighters make their way to the cage. Roman calls out two more fighters for the center ring and two more for the left. Once they're all inside, the cage doors are shut and locked. A part of me wants to close my eyes, to shut out the carnage I know is about to happen, but I can't.

Roman lifts the microphone and smiles. "Gentlemen, begin."

Growls echo in the underground lair, along with the sound of ripping flesh and snapping jaws. Blood permeates the air, and I hold my breath. It's going to be a very long day.

THE FIRST NINE fights went by quickly, but it was hard to stomach them all. No one backed down or submitted, which means I watched as nine men gave up their lives because of pride. After each fight, the blood was rinsed off the mats to get ready for the next round. There are three more fights to watch, which will finish up in the afternoon. Tate will be in one of them. I still have twelve more to endure tonight.

"In the center ring, I need Tate Grayson and Enrik Fenton."

Enrik enters the ring first, walking around arrogantly as if he's already won. Tate's not like that, and it's one of the things I love about him. He steps up into the ring, and Roman locks the cage door. Enrik bounces around, and Tate stands there all calm, like the silent killer I know he is.

"I'm sorry you have to see me this way," Tate says in my mind.

He looks over at me, and I smile sadly. *"You wouldn't be here if it wasn't for me. Whatever you do, I'll still love you. Nothing will make me see you differently."*

His glowing eyes turn to Enrik. *"That's what I needed to hear."*

All three cages have been locked, and all six fighters are ready. I hold my breath as Roman tells them to begin. The second he does, Enrik lunges for Tate. Tate moves out of the way with lightning speed. Enrik bolts around with a surprised look on his face.

Colin's mouth gapes. "Whoa. I didn't realize Grayson was so fast."

"There's a lot you don't know about him."

Micah moves in close. "The man makes it look effortless."

Enrik's anger builds as he continuously makes no gain on Tate. He shifts into his wolf, and Tate does the same, his shorts splitting into shreds. Both are giant gray wolves, but Tate is bigger. By the way Enrik backstepped, I don't think he was expecting Tate to be the size he is. They circle each other, baring their teeth. All eyes in the room are on them, even Killian, who watches them with fascination. I'm not too fond of the evil glint in his eyes; it's almost like he's thinking up a deceptive plan in that twisted mind of his.

Enrik hunches down low, preparing to strike. When he does, Tate's ready for him and latches onto his neck, delivering the killing blow. He tosses Enrik's lifeless body across the mat and shifts back into his human form, looking as if what he did was the easiest thing in the world.

Colin and Micah stand and cheer for him, but all I can think about is how he just became a target. Everyone will see him as a threat, especially Killian.

"I've already been a threat to him, love."

I glance over at Killian, and his eyes are solely on Tate. *"And now he knows it."*

Roman opens the cage door and lifts Tate's arm triumphantly. He won his first fight, but there are still plenty more. I have a feeling they'll be even more gruesome and horrific as the grand finale draws near.

TWENTY-EIGHT

FAITH

After the fights, Killian had a dinner prepared for us so Colin and Micah could mingle with the women in his pack. They weren't happy with me volunteering them to be displayed like pieces of meat, but there wasn't any other option. The dining room is full of Blue River pack women, fawning all over them. The guys smile and talk to them, but they aren't flirty like they are at home with other women.

Killian leaves Colin and Micah to sit with me at the-mile-long dining room table. It's the first time I've eaten a full meal since being in his company. Having Colin and Micah with me has helped. I don't feel so alone with them physically here and with Tate in my mind.

"It brings me comfort knowing you're in my mind too," Tate murmurs.

Looking down at my food, I smile.

Killian chuckles. "What are you smiling about?"

I nod over at Colin and Micah. "Them. I'm glad they're here."

Killian glances over at them. "Me too. Do you think they'll ever forgive me for taking you away?"

When I don't answer, he focuses on me. They would never forgive him, but I can't say that. "I don't know," I say. "They just want me to be happy. It's kind of hard when I'm left in limbo like this, all because of you."

His jaw clenches. "Most women like being fought for."

"If that's what you're used to, then yeah, maybe some do. But I'm not like that, Killian."

He sighs. "I get that now. I'm hoping one day *you* will forgive me."

The words that come out of his mouth sound genuine, but there's a darkness in his eyes that says otherwise. I believe Tia when she says he's always treated her kindly, and that's what makes this so complicated. Desperation can turn people into something they're not. Still, even if he's a good person underneath, it doesn't change the fact that he took me against my will.

Narrowing my gaze, I can feel my wolf just beneath the surface. I can see the reflection of my glowing eyes in his. "If an evil lunatic of a shifter wins this tournament, I will kill him before he can even think about being my mate. If any of the winners try to touch me during our time together, I will kill them. This is all your fault. I can't even think about forgiveness right now."

"Faith, what are you doing?" Tate demands.

"It's time I show everyone what I'm capable of." Tia's magic kept me from killing Killian that first night. He needs to see how lethal I can be, and the only way to do that is with the other wolves. Even they need to get a taste of how strong a shifter female can be.

Killian stares at me with wonder in his eyes. "I've been wondering when you were going to let your wolf out."

I scoff and grab my wine. "Yeah, she's kind of pissed right

now." I look over at Tia sitting in the corner, and she watches us curiously.

Killian moves in close, and I can feel Tate's anger vibrating through my body. "What if I won and let you go? Do you think you could forgive me then? I'll even give you half of the money."

The only way he could win is if Tate backs down or dies. Even if Tate weren't in the picture, I wouldn't believe him. "I don't want the money, Killian. I want my freedom."

"Then I'll give it to you. I know I can win. We just have to get through the next few days." He glances down at his phone and sighs. "It's time for me to go. I have to get ready for my fight."

I nod. "I'll be there."

Roman appears at the dining room door and nods for Killian to join him. Killian says his goodbyes to my brother and Micah before leaving the room. The women follow him out, leaving only me, Tia, Micah, and Colin.

Tia comes over to me and sits in the seat Killian just left. "That conversation was a little heated. What was it about?"

Micah and Colin walk over. "I was picking up on that too," Micah says, leaning against the table with his arms crossed.

I can't sense any wolves around, but that doesn't mean they aren't there. "Can we talk freely?" I ask Tia.

She nods. "Everyone's in the underground lair. Killian already told me to keep you all from escaping, so there's no way you could leave even if you wanted to. That's why he's comfortable leaving us alone. I was going to tell you earlier, but I couldn't."

"Of course," I hiss, throwing my arms in the air.

Colin huffs. "This fucking blows. What do we do now?"

I finish my wine and stand. "The only way to break this is to kill him. He asked me if I could forgive him for what he's done, and I said the only way I'd do that is if he let me go."

Tia gasps. "What did he say to that?"

I roll my eyes. "That'd he win and release me. He even said I could take half of the money."

Tia shakes her head. "He's not going to let you go, Faith. If anything, he's growing more attached to you. If I weren't taking away his violent and sexual urges, he'd have already forced himself on you. That's how bad it's getting."

If Tate was angry before, he's even more livid now. If I'd known Tia was going to say that, I would've blocked him.

"Don't shut me out, Faith. That'll piss me off even more."

Colin slams a hand down on the table, cracking the wood. "How else can this shit be broken?"

Tia glances over at me and closes her eyes. "You can either have Laila brought in to use her magic against me or ..." She blows out a shaky breath. "Or you can kill me." Her eyes clench like she's expecting a blow. When she opens her eyes, we all stare at her. They aren't going to kill her, and neither am I.

"We're not going to hurt you, Tia. That's not how we are. Bringing in Laila is out of the question. She's pregnant."

Tia's lips pull back in a sad smile. "I saw her in Wyoming, but she didn't see me. I'm happy for her."

Micah huffs. "We're back to square one."

Tia paces the floor. "We still have time to think." Howls echo outside, and she walks over to the window. "The fights are about to start. It's time to go."

Micah and Colin start for the door, but Tia grabs my arm, her expression torn. "What is it?" I ask her.

She looks into my eyes and sighs. "I have to warn you. Killian told me that once he gets in the cage tonight, I'm to release him. All of the rage he has will hit him full force."

I gasp. "Oh, my God."

She nods. "Exactly. He wants to intimidate the others. All

I can say is that it'll be one bloody mess. I honestly feel bad for the wolf he's fighting tonight."

"It won't be pretty," Tate informs me.

My stomach churns, and I swallow hard. Another wolf howls, and Tia takes my arm. "We have to go. It'll be over soon."

Not soon enough.

WE ALL WALK through the field to the building, and I can feel the raw energy before we even go through the door. Tia and I turn the corner first with Colin and Micah behind us. The more time I spend with Tia, the closer I feel to her. A part of me wonders if that's her plan or if she's using magic to make me believe everything she tells me.

"Trust your instincts, Faith," Tate murmurs.

Tia and I take our seats at the center ring. *"My instincts tell me to trust her."* But I still plan to stay on guard. Micah sits beside me, and Colin walks over to the chair beside Tia and sits down, which surprises me. She scans the room, but I keep my focus on the floor. I don't want to see any of the fighters just yet. Images of the earlier fights replay in my head, and I know what I'm about to see will be a million times worse than that.

"Hello, little wolf." The voice comes to my left, and I sigh. When I look over, I see Orin with a sly grin on his face. Judging by the way he's underdressed in only a pair of shorts like the other fighters, I assume that's what he's here for. He acknowledges Micah with a nod. "Protector."

Micah clenches his teeth and nods back, but he doesn't say anything.

"You're getting in the ring?" I ask Orin.

He shrugs as if it's no big deal. "Yeah. I figured I'd try my luck. I could make a pretty good mate."

If Orin wasn't in cahoots with Killian, I think I'd see him a lot differently. He has a sense of humor, and he seems like he'd be fun to be around. I hate he's throwing his life away for me.

"You have a mate out there somewhere, Orin. If you were smart, you'd wait for her."

Smile fading, he averts his gaze. "Some of us don't have that luxury." He nods at Tia and Colin and walks away.

"What's his story?"

I look at Tia, and her expression saddens. "Out of all the Blue River pack, Orin's my favorite. He always knows how to make me laugh. Before joining us, he was a rogue. He fell in love with a human and married her, only for her to die of cancer a couple of years ago. Her name was Rachel. When Killian found him in Ontario, he was in a bad way. He talked Orin into joining us here."

My heart breaks for him. I don't want to see him get killed because of me. "Is he seriously okay with fighting against Killian?"

Tia shrugs. "He knows it's a possibility. Honestly, I think he wants to lose. His heart is still broken."

"Is it sad that I want to save him?" I say to Tate in my mind.

"No, but you can't save someone who doesn't want to be saved," he replies.

Searching through the crowd, I find him standing by himself, stretching out his arms. *"I'm going to try."* One way or another, I'll find a way.

"You have got to be fucking kidding me," Colin hisses angrily. He jumps to his feet, and several of the shifters around us tense.

Heart racing, I stand and grab his arm. His energy puts

everyone close by on edge, and I don't want him in the middle of a brawl. "Hey, calm down. What's wrong?"

His eyes are fixed on someone across the room, and they're blazing. I follow his line of sight, and that's when I see what caught his attention. *Anson.* He's warming up in the corner, laughing and talking to a couple of other wolves.

Tate's confusion hits me first, but then his outright rage makes me stumble on my feet. Micah steadies me from behind. "Tate?"

So much is going through his mind, and all I see is red. The next thing I know, everything goes blank; he shut me out. "Yes," I whisper. "He blocked me."

Micah sighs. "He's got to be infuriated right now. It doesn't look like Anson's here against his will."

"No," I growl, my body trembling with the need to shift. "It doesn't." I storm through the crowd, and everyone gives me a wide berth, including the fighters. Colin and Micah are at my back, fuming just as much as I am. One of the shifters near Anson smacks his arm, and he turns in our direction. He tenses and looks away, but I'm not going to hold back. "You better look at me," I shout as I get closer. Colin grumbles something from behind, but I hold up a hand. "I got this." Anson's eyes flash when he looks at us, and I step right up to him. "What the hell are you doing here? We thought you were in trouble."

His attention shifts to someone over my shoulder, and I already know who it is. Killian moves up next to me and sighs. "It was a ruse, Faith. That's how I was able to find you. All it took was telling him about my plans for him to betray his alpha."

I don't take my eyes away from Anson. "Tate will never forgive you for this, and neither will I."

"Put me in the ring with him," Colin hisses, his voice husky and dark. "I'll make him suffer."

Anson throws up his hands, his gaze blazing like fire. "What the hell was I supposed to do, Faith? I asked Grayson to let you spend time with the pack to see if you could be a potential mate for one of us, but he kept you for himself. I wanted time with you."

I don't know Anson well, and he's not a part of my pack, but the betrayal runs deep. "And yet, you literally threw me to the wolves," I say. "I'm here because of you."

He shakes his head and looks away. "I didn't want to hurt you."

"Well, you did. What's worse is that you betrayed your alpha. I hope you're ready to face those consequences." He opens his mouth to speak, but I hold up a hand. "I'm done here. There's nothing left to say."

Turning on my heel, I walk away and take a deep breath. Tia waits for me by my seat, and I can see the anguish on her face. "I didn't want to be the one to tell you. I knew it would break your heart."

Micah huffs. "My concern is Tate. He's going to be livid."

"He'll be more than that," I whisper, feeling Tate come back into my mind. He stopped blocking me, but his thoughts are still flashes of red. *"Talk to me, Tate. Tell me you're okay."*

"I can't," he says, his voice rough and raw. *"He'll die for this."*

"I know." And I have the sinking suspicion that Killian's going to make sure Tate fights against Anson at some point.

Roman climbs up into the ring with his microphone and taps it. "All right, it looks like we started this night off with a little bit of excitement. Well, it's about to get even more exhilarating." He calls out the first four fighters who take their places in the left and right cages. I've noticed a trend with the center ring. It's where the most brutal fights have been.

"Prepare yourself," Tia whispers. "Killian's going in." Roman calls out his name and his opponents. Killian steps into the ring, all calm and collected, just like Tate did. The other guy paces around, his eyes already glowing a bright shade of green. The energy in the room skyrockets, and Tia grabs my hand, her skin running ice cold. Her breathing runs rapid, and she sucks in a breath as it hurts to breathe. "He wants to be unleashed. I can't fight it."

Roman locks the cage door, and Killian's opponent shifts. He turns his glowing eyes onto Tia, and within seconds, all hell breaks loose. His wolf bursts free, and he bashes into the other wolf, slamming him into the cage. Blood splatters all over the mat as he rips his opponent in half. Killian's men hoot and holler from the sidelines, cheering on their alpha as he decimates the wolf, limb from limb. I'm mortified, but I can't look away—Killian's like a rabid animal, high off of blood and gore. I've never been terrified of another wolf, but Killian is what nightmares are made out of.

"Were you prepared for that?" Tia asks.

I shake my head. "Not at all."

Looking around at the crowd, neither was anyone else.

TWENTY-NINE

TATE

I don't know if it's the anger from Anson's betrayal or if the rage is starting to set in. Hell, it could be both. All I know is that I feel like I'm losing control. With Faith being in Killian's clutches and me not being able to be with her is taking its toll. I can't stand not being able to protect her. What's worse is that I have no fucking clue how I will make it out of this alive.

In less than an hour, I'll be back in the ring, fighting for my mate. It's kill or be killed. I have no choice. As I'm looking out the window, the small town seems a lot quieter now. What started as forty-eight men is now down to twenty-four. After today, there will only be twelve.

Sitting on the hotel bed, I look down at my cell, dreading what I'm about to tell my father. We've never had someone in our pack betray us the way Anson has. I press send, and it only rings once before my father picks up.

"Tate," he says, his voice sounding desperate. "Thank God, you're okay."

I look over at the alarm clock on the dresser. There are

only ten minutes before Killian's men will be picking me up at the abandoned shack. "I'm far from it," I tell him.

"What's going on, son?"

"Anson betrayed us, Dad. He's the one who told Vilkas that Faith and I were in Florida."

My father growls. "Son of a bitch." He already knows about the fights and what I'm up against. The news about Anson is going to change our pack forever. "Have you talked to him?"

I huff. "Faith did. She confronted him last night, and I heard everything through our bond. He was mad because I refused to share Faith with the pack. He saw this as his chance to win her." When I close my eyes, I can see the smug look on his face. There's no remorse. No guilt for what he did. My body trembles with the need to shift.

"They're going to pair you up with him, son. You know that, right?"

"I know," I say, sighing heavily. "I doubt it'll be today. He'll make it through to the top four."

"And when he does. What are you going to do?"

Visions of me ripping him apart flash through my mind. "I'll kill him. There's no forgiving him after this."

"No, there's not," my dad agrees. "He has to pay the price."

"He will, but I don't know if it's going to do any good. I know I'll make it to the final round, but it'll be against Vilkas. His witch will make sure I lose."

"If anyone can get out of this, it's you, Tate. You're smart and stronger than any man I know, including me. I often wonder how I got so lucky to have a son like you."

Time is ticking by. I look out the window once more before leaving the room. "If I don't make it out alive, you need to keep the pack together."

"Don't worry about us, son. You're going to be fine.

Everyone will be waiting for you to come back with your mate."

We say our goodbyes, and I head out of the hotel toward the edge of town. Three other shifters are waiting at the shack. Two of them weren't in my fighting group yesterday, but I recognize them through Faith's mind. The third one, however, fought in my group. His name is Dixon, and he's an arrogant tool. I'd love to fight him.

"You don't talk much, do you?" he says to me.

I stare right at him, unleashing some of the power I keep hidden inside of me. "Maybe it's because I have nothing to say to you."

His jaw clenches, and he backs off. The other two do the same, giving me a wide berth. Killian's men arrive a few minutes later, and we all get in the van, none of them saying a word.

"I'm ready to see you," Faith murmurs in my mind.

"I'm ready to see you too. I just wish it wasn't like this."

"Me too. I want it to be over, but I know we need the time to figure out what to do. Tia's link to Killian is dangerous. She can't control what he makes her do. He says he'll let me go if he wins, but it means you lose for him to do that. Not a single bone in my body trusts him."

I clench my fists tight. *"You shouldn't. If he wins, he's not going to let you go."*

Her silence says everything. I'm glad she doesn't believe any of the shit Killian tells her. There's only one way to break through Tia's magic, and it's to complete the bond. The full moon is only five days away, but it's also the night of the final fight. Getting alone time with Faith isn't going to happen.

We pull up to the gate, and it opens. The driver takes us right to the building and slides the van door to the side. Dixon and the other two shifters stay put, so I get out first. Roman walks toward me and smiles. "You missed some of the excitement last night."

"Yeah, I heard," I say, keeping my anger in check.

He flourishes a hand toward the door. "Go on down. Everyone's warming up."

By everyone, I assume it means Anson is already there. I walk inside the building to the back hallway and then down the stairs to the underground pit. When I turn the corner, silence fills the air. After Faith's altercation with Anson, everyone surely knows the truth about how she got here. If any of the shifters here were honorable, they'd try to figure out a way to get Faith out after learning she was kidnapped for Killian's fucked up tournament. But are they helping? No. All they see is power and a beautiful mate for the taking. It's that kind of knowledge that makes me not regret killing any of them.

I scan the room, and that's when I see the traitorous bastard standing on the opposite side of the room, talking to three men of the Blue River pack.

"Tate, don't," Faith warns.

"I'm sorry, love. I have to." With Anson in my sights, I shut my mind off from hers. She doesn't need to see or hear any of the thoughts running through my mind. Everyone moves out of the way, giving me a clear path. Anson has his back to me, and when he stiffens, I know he knows I'm there.

When he turns around, I don't waste any time. I punch him so hard his head snaps to the side, his blood splattering across the wall.

He slowly turns to me and laughs as blood pours out of his nose. "I was expecting worse."

I knew I wouldn't get far with all of Killian's men in the room. There are at least six of them at my back and three slowly making their way to Anson. "Oh, believe me, you'll get it," I snarl.

Anson shrugs. "I wouldn't be here if it wasn't for you. You got greedy."

Roman steps in between us. "All right, men. That's enough." His eyes meet mine. "Step away, Grayson."

As I glance over my shoulder, there are now eight men ready to pull me back. Killian stands off to the side of the room, clearly amused by the smirk on his face. Clenching my teeth, I hold up my hands. "I'm done." Fire burning through my veins, I glare at Anson. "You better hope they don't put us in the ring together."

Anson grins, which only infuriates me more. "Oh, I'll be ready. I can promise you that."

So will I.

THIRTY

I t's only the second day of the fights, and it feels like I've watched them for years. Killian fought first, and it was no surprise he won. I feared he'd have Tate fight against Anson, but they both had different opponents. They won their fights, of course. Anson's fighting technique is remarkably similar to Tate's.

"That's because we learned to fight together," Tate says in my mind.

I look over at him, sitting alone across the room. Inside his mind is a whirlwind of thoughts and emotions. I want to go over there and touch him just once, but I'm so afraid everyone will see right through us and know we're mates.

Micah nudges me with his elbow. "Come on. I'll walk you over there. He's getting ready to have to leave." Tia nods for me to go and she stays put with Colin right beside her. Tate stands when we draw near, and it takes all I have not to run into his arms.

"It's hard for me too, love."

Micah squeezes his shoulder reassuringly. "You're doing good."

Tate smiles, and it's such a welcome sight. "I'm trying."

Micah glances around the room. "There's not many of you left."

"Grayson, it's time to go," Roman shouts.

A low growl rumbles from Tate's chest, but he bites his tongue. He looks at me with those bright blue eyes of his, and I give in. Throwing my arms around his neck, I close my eyes and breathe him in.

"I don't want to let you go." My eyes burn, but I hold back the tears. Seeing him leave gets harder each time.

His grip on me tightens. *"Neither do I."*

When I let him go, Roman and three of Killian's other men are ready to take him away. "Be safe," I whisper.

Tate nods. "I will."

As soon as he walks out of the room, it feels empty. Micah latches onto my arm, his voice a little lower than a whisper. "Let me call Cedric and Laila. She can get us out of this."

I'm starting to wonder if that is our only hope. Laila has some powerful friends among the fae, but I can't expect them to go out of their way to help me. I don't have ties to them. It'll be left up to Laila herself. "That'll be our last resort. Until then, we need to figure out our own way. I'll never forgive myself if something happened to her or the baby."

"I know," he agrees. "I don't want that either."

Tia and Colin are over by Killian, but they leave him to come to us. My brother is my eyes and ears on the inside. So far, he's had nothing to report. Tia smiles at me, and I can tell it's forced. Out of the corner of my eye, I can see Killian watching us. "Killian wants to know if he can see you tonight. After everything going on, I'm sure he'll understand if you're too tired, though." Colin's back is to Killian, and when I look up at him, he mouths the words *say you're tired.*

"Actually, I am exhausted. I'd really like to go to bed," I say.

Tia nods, and I can see the relief on her face. "I'll let him know." She walks off toward him while Colin and Micah escort me out of the underground pit.

"Good choice," Colin says as we walk out into the fresh air.

I snort. "If only I could use that excuse every time." Eventually, Killian won't take no as an answer.

MIDNIGHT HAS COME AND GONE, and I'm still wide awake. I'm so afraid that if I go to sleep, something will happen, and I'll never hear Tate's voice again.

"I'm right here, Faith," Tate murmurs, sounding as if he's right beside me.

When I close my eyes, I can almost imagine he is. *"One day, we need to travel to Aruba or the Turks and Caicos. I hear the snorkeling is amazing."*

Our future is uncertain, but it feels good to think about how things could be. Tate chuckles in my head, and it brings a smile to my face. *"One of my friends and his wife just got back from the Turks and Caicos a couple of months ago. They said the food was awesome."*

"All right, it's settled then. We'll go there."

"Sounds good, love. I quite like seeing you in a bikini." Our time in Florida will always hold a special place in my heart. I'd give anything to feel him inside of me again. *"Trust me, Faith. I'd give anything to feel that too."* A click at the door makes me gasp, and I bolt out of bed. *"Faith, what's going on?"*

"I think someone's trying to come into my room. It could be Micah or Colin. But if not, someone's about to have a terrible night." I tiptoe to the door and rest my back against the wall. The door opens slightly, and Tia sticks her head in.

"Faith, it's just me."

"Jesus," I huff, opening the door the rest of the way. "What the hell are you doing?"

She sneaks in, wearing a pair of flannel pajama pants and a T-shirt. "I wanted to talk to you."

I flip on the lights and walk over to the bed. "Where's Killian?" I ask.

"Asleep," she says, shutting the door behind her. She comes over to the bed and sits on the edge. "I had to wait until it was safe to talk." Her eyes close, and she chants a few words under her breath. When her eyes open, it's as if everything comes to life around me. Before, I couldn't feel a single shifter nearby because she had hidden them. Now I can sense them all, including Killian. No one is around. "I can't stay long, but I had to warn you. Killian's impatience grows stronger by the day. It's getting harder to control him."

Her words send shivers down my spine. "What happens if you can't?"

Fear runs through her eyes. "I don't know. I'm hoping we don't find out. I wanted to warn you earlier, but there were too many ears around."

I don't want to think about what's on my mind, but I can't help it. "So, if Killian were to force himself on me, your magic would keep me from overpowering him." It's not a question but a statement.

"Holy fucking shit, I will lose my mind if that happens. Nothing and no one will be able to stop me from ripping through the front gate to get to you," Tate thunders.

Tia averts her gaze. "Yes. I'm doing everything I can to make sure that doesn't happen. He hasn't been with a woman in a long time. There isn't a lot of options here in Baker's Ridge. Humans are too fragile, and he doesn't want any of the women in his pack."

Unmated males who experience the rage let out their frustrations with sex, mainly with human women. If Killian's been suppressing those urges for that long, he's a ticking time bomb waiting to explode.

"Great," I grumble. "Just what I wanted to hear."

"He better not fucking touch you," Tate snaps.

Tia blows out a sigh. "Tomorrow, there will be three fights. Tate's not in this group, but Killian is. The three winners will get to spend an hour alone with you. It's up to you on what you'd like to do in that hour."

The mention of Tate catches my attention. "Why did you mention Tate Grayson?"

Her brows furrow. "He's your friend, right? Plus, I've seen how you are when he fights. You care for him."

"I do. Tate's a good person."

Her eyes never waver from mine. "Is he your mate, Faith?"

"No," I answer in all seriousness. "We're just friends." I feel like I can trust her, but I'm not ready to disclose my secrets.

"Speaking of friends," she mentions. "When you were in Wyoming and staying with Laila and Cedric, there was something else blocking me other than her fae magic. I didn't tell Killian what it was, but I have my suspicions."

"And what are they?"

She nods at me. "That when your kind finds their true mates, you become indestructible. Outside magic won't work on you because you're stronger."

"You're right," I confess. "We do become a force to be reckoned with. It's one of the perks of finding your true mate. I don't think those same rules apply when a mating is forced. The goddess of the moon doesn't reward evil." It's times like now I wish that Killian could hear everything I say. Yes, my power would join with his if we were to mate, but it won't be as strong as my bond with Tate. Tia stares off into space, and I wave my hand in front of her face. "You still in there?"

She blows out a sigh. "Yeah, sorry. Just thinking."

"About what?" I question. I can tell the wheels in her mind are turning.

"I don't know yet, but I'm hoping it comes to me soon." She slides off my bed and goes to the door. She stops and glances at me over her shoulder. "One of these days, I hope you can learn to trust me, Faith. I really do want to help you."

I don't know what to say, so I say nothing at all. A look of disappointment passes across her face when she walks out. I expect her to block me from Killian and his men like she had before, but she doesn't. I can sense where every single one of them are.

"Maybe that's her attempt at hoping I trust her?" I say to Tate.

"It's a start. At least now you know who's around. No one can sneak up on you."

It does make things easier.

I lay down in bed, and my disappointment grows. *"I'm not going to see you tomorrow."*

Tate's frustration grows through our bond. *"I know. It makes me sick to think of you in the same house as Vilkas. What if he loses control around you? Your brother and Micah won't be able to kill him."*

It's something I refuse to think about.

"Please, let's not talk about it. I need something happy in my life right now. Tell me about all the places you've been to. Don't leave out any details. I want to see it in my mind."

And just like that, I can see a whole new world in my head. Tate takes me through all of his adventures, and it feels like I'm right there. It's my only escape from the hell I'm in.

THIRTY-ONE

FAITH

It's Monday. Four days until the full moon. Usually, when people count down days like that it's for a happy event, but not for me. Killian brought me breakfast this morning, saying how he wished he could've spent time with me last night. His demeanor was different, like he's holding on by a thread. I made sure not to provoke him for fear of what he'd do. He went over the itinerary and who all were fighting today. I listened and kept most of my comments to myself. The three winners will get one on one time with me. At first, I was not too fond of the idea, but I can turn it into something useful, depending on who the winners are.

With Anson being one of the contenders, I told Killian if he wins his fight, he might not survive the hour with her. Unfortunately, it's not my place to dole out his punishment. Tate has that right more than anyone.

"If you feel the need to kill him, be my guest," Tate says. *"He betrayed you just as much as he did me."*

It's strange having fewer people in the underground pit. Before, it was filled with shifters, but now there are only six fighters with the Blue River pack as the audience. Out of the six men, I already know Killian, Anson, and Orin will be the winners. They're the strongest. While they get ready for their fights, I watch Killian's pack members.

The women still vie for Colin and Micah's attention, but I think they know nothing will happen between them. I can see the disappointment in their eyes. It's easy to see why they would let Killian organize fights to find them a mate. Everyone wants to feel loved and wanted. My heart hurts for them. They can't help it their alpha is losing his mind to the rage.

Tate's sigh sounds sad in my head. *"You can't save everyone, Faith."*

"No, but I can try."

Now that there are only three fights, each one is being done individually instead of three at one time like the past two days. Tia sits beside me like she has every other time, dressed in a sexy blue dress today, and leans in but keeps her eyes on the center ring. It's time for Killian to fight.

"We need to talk. It's important."

I can hear the urgency in her voice. "Okay," I whisper.

"After the fights, say you need to go to your room to freshen up. That might give me enough time."

My curiosity piques. By her tone, I can't tell if it's good or bad news. Anything would be better than bad news at this point. Roman steps out of the ring, leaving Killian and a shifter named Penn from Alberta to fight it out. We all know how this is going to go. I half expect Penn to give up when Killian shifts into his wolf, but he doesn't. Pride is a dangerous thing among my kind, and it's going to cost Penn his life.

It takes ten full minutes of hardcore fighting for Killian to deliver the final blow. Out of all the fighters who were paired against Killian, Penn was the strongest. Next up is Anson, and I already know he's going to win by the gleam in his eyes as he stalks the other wolf around the ring. I can't believe I never saw the darkness in him before.

"Do you think he would've betrayed you if he knew we were mates?" I ask Tate.

I can feel Tate in my mind, but it takes him a while to respond. *"I wish I knew. It's almost like he's a different person right now. I'm starting to think he would've ratted us out so that I couldn't have you."*

Anson defeats his opponent and shifts back into his human form, lifting his head triumphantly. I look away because I can't stand the thought of acknowledging his win. Soon, I'll have to spend an hour with him alone. It'll be the perfect chance to tell him how I feel about him.

Roman calls Orin up to the ring and his opponent. Out of all the men besides Tate, I have a soft spot for Orin. I already know the final fight will be between Tate and Killian, which means someone will end up killing Orin. I don't want to watch it happen.

Tia flinches every time Orin gets hit but then smiles when he wins. Deep down, I'm happy he's the victor too. *"You care too much,"* Tate murmurs. *"I know what you're thinking with Orin. Don't get discouraged if he doesn't listen."*

"I'm going to make him hear me out." I have a plan.

Orin steps out of the ring and stands between Killian and Anson. Roman comes over to me and flourishes a hand toward them. "Here are your three winners. You get an hour with each of them. Who do you want to be first?"

"Orin," I say. "Then Anson, and then Killian." Orin looks at me, and I nod toward the exit. "I'm going to my room to change, so meet me up at the house when you're ready."

He nods and smiles but doesn't say anything. Killian seems all too happy to be chosen last by the sly grin on his face, but I try not to think about what he has on his mind. Colin and Micah flank me, and we follow Tia out of the underground pit. I'm ready to get to my room to find out what she needed to say.

We get to the house, and there are no wolves inside, only

three around the perimeter. As soon as we're upstairs and in my room, she shuts the door. Colin and Micah both look at me, confused. "What's going on?" Colin asks.

Tia comes up to me and grabs my hands, pulling me close to her. "Tell me, Faith. Are you and Tate true mates?"

I keep my eyes on her because if she sees me look at Colin and Micah, she'll know I'm lying. I want to tell her, yes, but I can't. "No, we're not," I say, lying straight to her face.

Her face falls, and she closes her eyes. "That's not what I wanted to hear." She lets me go and turns for the door.

"What does it matter?" I ask.

She stops at the door but doesn't turn to look at me. "I had an idea, but it doesn't matter. I'll figure something else out."

"Tell me," I demand.

On the floor below us, one of Killian's shifters walks into the house. Tia opens the door and walks out, leaving me to wonder what the hell she was talking about.

"I want to know what she was going to tell me," I say, keeping my voice low. What if it was something that could help us?

"Do you really want to tell her the truth?" Micah asks. I don't know what I want to do.

MICAH AND COLIN left so I could change clothes and get ready to meet Orin. It doesn't take him long to come to the house, and when he does, I meet him downstairs in the foyer. His light, ashy brown hair is still a little damp from his shower, and he has on a pair of jeans and a flannel shirt. He greets me with a smile, and it's hard not to return one to him.

"What do you want to do, little wolf?" he asks.

Everything Tia told me about him and his lost love makes my heart break. "I want to go for a walk around the gardens."

He holds out his arm. "Let's go then."

I take his arm, and I can feel Tate in my mind, but he doesn't say anything, even though I can feel his displeasure with Orin touching me. Orin and I walk around the side of the house to the gardens. Even though I despise Killian, I can't hate his gardens; it's a paradise for me.

"I already know a lot about you," Orin begins, "but I'm sure there's a lot I don't. Tell me something you don't think I'd know."

Letting his arm go, I bend down and run a finger over the bright pink flowers. "Micah and I have a landscaping business. Did you know that?"

Orin chuckles. "No, I didn't. I do, however, know you paint. I saw some of your work in the Jackson Hole gallery."

Pursing my lips, I look up at him. "Oh, you mean, when you were busy stalking me?"

He holds up his hands. "Not one of my finest moments."

Standing, I reach for his arm again. "Have you always lived in this part of Canada?" I ask, knowing he hasn't.

His smile falters. "No. I was born in Ontario. I've only been with the Blue River pack for two years."

It kills me to drag this out. "Okay," I say, standing in front of him. His eyes widen, and I hold up a hand. "I don't want to lie to you. Just listen to what I have to say."

He cocks his head to the side. "What are you doing?"

I take a deep breath and blow it out. "Drop out of the tournament."

"Why?" He's taken aback by my statement.

My heart pounds in my chest. "Because you don't belong here. I've seen the men who are fighting for me, and none of them are like you." Taking his hands, I squeeze them hard. "You're a good person, Orin. You may be a smartass at times, but I like you. Deep down, you know I'm not your mate."

He shakes his head. "You don't know that."

"Yes, I do." I move closer to him and stare right into his eyes. "You know it too. I know you lost someone you loved."

His eyes flash, and he looks away, but I hold tight on his hands. "Who told you that?"

"Tia did. She's worried about you and so am I." Closing my eyes, I concentrate on our surroundings to make sure no one's close by to hear us. When I open them, Orin's still looking away. I take his chin and turn him back to me. "You know the outcome of this tournament, Orin. If sacrificing yourself to get rid of the heartbreak is what you really want to do, do it. Honestly, I don't think that's what Rachel would want."

His eyes flash, and he closes them. "I haven't heard her name in a long time."

Letting his chin go, I hold his hands again. "Look at me." When he opens his eyes, I can see the pain. "I don't know what's going to happen when this tournament ends, but I can promise you that I will do everything I can to help you find your mate. She's out there, waiting for *you*. You will be able to love again. Your mate will make you whole."

He shakes his head. "What if I'm not worthy? I've done too many bad things in the past two years. Look what I've done to you. You're stuck here against your will."

I squeeze his hands. "I forgive you for that. If you start doing things the right way, you'll find your redemption. I have faith in that."

He chuckles. "Faith has faith."

"I do," I say with a smile. "And right now, I have all the faith in the world that you'll make the right decision."

With a heavy sigh, he looks at me with regret. "Okay. I'll back out. You're going to need a friend here once all of this is over."

I don't want to think about that just yet. Swallowing hard, I hug him. "Thank you. I promise you won't regret it." I let him go and nod toward the gardens. "Come on. We still have some time left."

Orin smiles. "At least our time together is nice. I pity Anson. Do you think you can be alone with him without killing him?"

That's a good question. "I don't know," I answer honestly. "But I'm about to find out."

ONCE MINE and Orin's time came to a close, he left to find Anson. I chose Killian's library as our alone destination for a reason. One, I love books, and they always make me happy. Killian's library is two stories tall and filled with literature from top to bottom. Being in here reminds me of Belle in *Beauty and the Beast*, only I'm not going to fall in love with the beast. And two, I'd have something to throw at Anson if he says something to piss me off.

"Throw the books hard," Tate says.

"Oh, I will."

Anson draws closer, and I toss the last book I need on the desk. When he walks in, he looks around, confused. "Why the library?" he asks, clearly disappointed.

Glaring at him, I beckon him closer with a wave of my hand. "I thought you might like to read these." He moves closer, and I fling the first book at him, and it hits him in the chest. "That one's called *Betrayed*." I throw another one at him. "*Stabbed in the Back*." The next book I have aimed straight for his head, but he ducks. "That one was titled *The Knives Come Out*. Do you get the message here?"

Anson stalks toward me. "I get it loud and clear. It doesn't change anything."

I throw my hands in the air. "Why are you even still in the

competition? I would never agree to be your mate after what you did to Tate."

He shrugs. "It's not up to you, now is it? You don't have a choice." His eyes flash, and he comes closer, making the hair on the back of my neck stand on end. I back up until I'm flush against the bookshelves with nowhere to go.

"Motherfucker," Tate growls. *"Is anyone around to help you?"*

"I don't need help. I got this."

Anson blocks me in and glances up and down my body. "I've been thinking about what it'd be like to mate with you, to feel those legs of yours wrapped around my waist as I fuck you senseless."

Tate's rage explodes through my mind. Clenching my teeth, I can feel my nails and fangs lengthen. "I'll kill you before you can even touch me."

He lifts a hand, and I grab his neck, sinking my claws into his skin. His eyes widen, and he gasps in shock. All I'd have to do is dig my nails in more and tear his head off. The library door bursts open, and Colin and Micah rush in, followed by Killian. They all stare at me in disbelief. I want Killian and Anson to know I have the power to kill them.

Anson gurgles blood, and I lean in close to whisper in his ear. "I do have a choice, you pathetic jackass. I could've killed you just now, but I didn't. Let that sink in."

I push him away, and he grabs his neck, the blood slowing as he heals. Killian glares at him and points to the door. "Get out."

Anson hurries out the door, and Colin starts after him. "Colin, don't," I shout.

He clenches his fists and turns his anger to Killian. "See what you've done? This never would've happened if it wasn't for you."

Micah rushes over to me. "Are you okay?"

I nod, but Tate's anger is suffocating me. "I'm fine."

Killian glances down at my blood-stained hands. "You should've killed him. You had every right."

Tate shuts off his mind from me, and I breathe a sigh of relief. "I'm okay."

Micah stares at me in wonder. "I never thought I'd see the day. You looked pretty damn lethal."

"Now he knows I have the power and the strength to kill him." My words are for Killian, but I keep my eyes on Micah.

Micah nods. "Yes, you do."

The room falls silent, but then I turn my attention to Killian, who steps out of my way. "Let me get cleaned up, and then we can meet for our hour." Showing my full strength to Anson gave me a high I've never felt before. It's empowering. I walk out of the library, and two of Killian's men quickly move to the side. A scent fills the air, and I breathe it in ... fear. They're afraid of me.

Good.

THIRTY-TWO

FAITH

Time ticks further on by. It's now Tuesday, three days till the full moon, and we still don't know how we're going to defeat Killian. Tate is here, and he won his fight, along with two other shifters, Dixon and Alister. During my hour with Dixon, I learned he's an arrogant ass. No amount of persuading him was going to get him to back out of the tournament. Alister, however, was a different story. I wasn't able to convince him to back out, but I did coerce him into a bet. He wouldn't fight me because he heard what I did to Anson, but he did agree to a race. If I won, he would back out. If he won, I'd have to spend an extra two hours with him. We raced in front of everyone, and he lost. I'm glad I was able to save two people out of the forty-eight. Orin kept to his word and told Killian he wanted out.

Now it's time for my hour with Tate. It feels like it's been an eternity since I've touched him. I stand in the gardens, waiting not so patiently for Tate to walk out of the building.

"You sure are taking forever," I say in his mind.

"I'm coming. I have to wait for these fuckers to walk me out.

They're talking about the women in town they're going to fuck tonight. Killian's taking them out to celebrate."

"Celebrate? He hasn't won yet."

"True. Vilkas gets cockier the closer we get to the end."

A few minutes later, he walks out of the building with three wolves following behind him. Once he's halfway, they stand back, and he finishes the rest of the way by himself. I don't care who's around, but I throw my arms around him.

"We have an hour. What do you want to do?"

He hugs me. *"I can think of plenty. Making love to you would be my first choice."*

"That would be nice."

"I don't know," he says out loud since there are wolves within hearing distance. "Guess you could show me around?"

I take his arm. "I'd be happy to." We walk around the gardens, even though he's seen it all through my mind.

"Nice job challenging that moron to a race. You surprised everyone when you beat him."

I tighten my hold on his arm. "That was fun. If only I could've spent time with the other fighters. Maybe some of them would still be alive."

"You can't blame yourself for that. They chose to do this." We head around the side of the house to the front entrance. Killian and Roman walk out just as we're about to enter.

Killian holds out a hand to Tate. "Good fight today, Grayson."

Tate shakes his hand. "Thanks."

Killian focuses on me. "I'm going into town for a while tonight. If you need anything, you have my number."

The further he's away from me, the better. "Have fun."

He looks at Tate one more time. "Barrett and Wilson will be taking you back shortly." They walk off, and we watch them get into his expensive Mercedes and drive down to the gate.

"Faith," Micah calls out, his tone urgent. I turn toward the door, and he waves for us to follow him. "I need you and Tate, now."

He runs up the stairs, and we follow him. "Micah, what's wrong?"

When we get into my room, Colin and Tia are in there. Micah shuts the door and sighs. "There's something you need to hear."

The grave expressions on Tia and Colin's faces make my stomach clench with dread. "Go on," I say.

Tia paces my room, her face pale. "Killian finally told me his plans for the full moon."

Tate tenses beside me, and both Colin and Micah look as if they could kill someone. "And?" I ask, barely recognizing the sound of my voice.

A tear falls down her cheek when she meets my eyes. "And he wants me to subdue you so you two can complete the bond after he wins the main fight. That way, once you're mates, there's nothing you can do." It's what I feared and refused to think about. Tia breaks down and cries. "I can't stop myself from doing that to you, Faith. It makes me sick to think of him taking advantage of you like that."

Tate's rage fills the room. "We have no choice. We have to call in Laila and Cedric. Her magic is the only thing that can save us."

Tia shakes her head. "There's another way." We all stare at her, and by the sorrow filtering out of her, I know I'm not going to like what she has to say. She turns to Micah and Colin. "I've tried breaking the link before, and the pain was excruciating. I can try again, but if it doesn't work ..." She stops mid-sentence, her lips trembling.

"If it doesn't work, then what?" I ask.

She takes a deep breath. "Then I need someone to kill me. It's the only way you'll defeat Killian."

Colin and Micah both shake their heads. "No," I shout.

"That's not going to happen." She paces the room faster, and I grab her shoulders to stop her. When she looks into my eyes, there's a vulnerability in hers I've never seen before. I'm starting to think it's time I trust her. "When you came in here the other night asking if Tate was my mate, you seemed to have a plan for that."

Nodding, she wipes away her tears. "I did, but you were adamant that he's not." I glance over at Tate, and he nods. Tia's eyes widen, and she huffs. "So he is, isn't he? I had a feeling you didn't fully trust me."

"Can you blame me?" I counter.

She laughs sadly. "No. I would've done the same thing."

Tate steps forward. "Tell us this plan. How does me being Faith's mate help us?"

Tia's smile widens. "You can thank your good friend, Laila, for this." She pulls out two light blue stones from her pocket. "I've kept these with me just in case. I had a feeling Faith wasn't being completely honest with me. I wanted to be prepared." Laila was a master at using various stones for their magical properties. Tia places a stone in both Tate and Micah's palms and closes a hand over them. With her eyes closed, she whispers a chant. When she opens her eyes, she steps back and smiles.

Colin gasps. "Holy fuck. What the hell happened?"

I look over at Tate, but instead of it being him, he looks like Micah. When I turn to my left where Micah was standing, he now appears to be Tate. Tia giggles and pulls me to her side so that I face the guys. "It's a glamour, Faith. As long as the guys carry the stones, they'll appear to be the other." She takes the stone away from Tate, and instead of looking like Micah, his true self appears. The same goes for Micah. He no longer looks like Tate when he gives up the stone.

Tia turns me to face her. "Micah and Tate can switch places. There are always loopholes in magic. Micah can leave as Tate and Tate can stay here with you. They'll just have to switch back before Tate's next fight. That is if the guys don't mind."

Micah slaps a hand on Tate's shoulder. "I'll do it, brother. You two have been separated long enough."

Tate gives him a side hug. "I'm in your debt."

Colin clears his throat. "This is all nice and all, but how's this going to help us with Vilkas? Tate will still be under your magic during the final fight."

We all look at Tia, and she brightens. "The full moon begins at sunset and lasts until sunrise the next morning. Killian wants the fight at midnight, the peak of when shifters are the strongest." She steps forward and takes our hands. "You may not have hours to enjoy mated bliss, but if you can complete your bond right at sunset, then you'll have all the power you need. My magic won't work on you because you'll be stronger." She smiles up at Tate. "You'll be a royal. You can defeat Killian and put an end to all of this. I'll get my freedom."

"And I'll get mine," I murmur. "To think we almost missed out on this chance."

Tia squeezes my hand. "It's not over yet. We still don't know who's fighting against who tomorrow. If Killian wants it to be Tate, then we're screwed. There are only four fighters left."

Tate's jaw clenches. "If Killian fights Dixon tomorrow, that leaves Anson for me."

Tia lets our hands go, and I wrap my arms around Tate's waist. "I'm sorry."

He leans down and kisses me. "He's the one who'll be sorry. No one touches my mate and gets away with it."

Two wolves approach the house, and their footsteps pound on the floor beneath us. Tia hands the stones back to Micah and Tate. I turn to the real Micah and stare into his eyes which are now Tate's. "Thank you for this. I love you so much."

He hugs me quickly. "You better. Stay safe."

"I will."

The door opens and Barrett glares at who he assumes is Tate. "Let's go, Grayson."

Micah winks at me and follows Barrett out the door. I hurry to the window and watch them leave through the gate. There are only two wolves on the property, but they're on the far end where the building is.

"Where is everyone?"

Tia snorts. "In town. Killian knows you can't go anywhere. That's why he only has two men protecting the compound and two for the house. Plus, he knows there's nothing romantic going on between you and Micah. He doesn't mind you two being alone together." She smiles and nods toward Tate who is talking to Colin. "You can always take advantage of this alone time. Especially with Barrett and Wilson taking Micah into town."

Tate hears her, and Colin backs away to the door. "That's my cue to leave." Tate sets the stone on my dresser, and Micah's body fades away.

Tia smiles at us both. "Have fun, you two." She walks out and shuts the door behind her.

Tate's need hits me like a ton of bricks. "We may only have a few minutes," I say, my heart racing out of control.

His eyes flash. "That's all we need." He rips off his clothes, and I barely get mine off before he tosses me onto the bed. His lips lock onto mine, demanding and hot as he tastes me. I give in to him, loving the feel of him claiming me. "I want you so fucking bad right now."

I want him too, more than I've wanted anything else in the world. His hands are everywhere, caressing my skin, and I do the same to him. I can't get enough. "You have no idea how much I've missed you." All he has to do is feel between my legs to know how much. My thighs are wet, and my body screams at me to let him inside.

A groan rumbles in his chest, and he licks his lips. Crawling up my body, he spreads my legs with his hands, his gaze on mine as he slides his tongue across my clit. Everything inside of me tightens, and I suck in a breath. He plunges in deep, breathing me in as he tastes me. My orgasm hits me from the inside out, and when my hips lift, he holds me to his face. Biting my lip to keep from screaming, I ride wave after wave of ecstasy. Tate groans and slides his tongue inside me one more time.

"You taste so fucking good. I wish I could do this every day."

I giggle. "Trust me. I'd let you." With his heated gaze on mine, he kisses his way up my thighs to my stomach. His hands clutch my breasts, and one after the other, he pulls my nipples between his teeth and sucks them generously—my back arches off the bed, desperate for him to suck harder.

"As you wish," Tate says in my mind.

He gets into position and pushes his hardness inside of me while ravishing my nipples. I suck in a breath as he fills me completely, thrusting his hips gently yet deep. I never knew I could need someone as much as I needed him. His touch sends fire through my veins. Gripping me gently, he flips us over, and I'm now on top. I can feel him stretching me, the ache of it so blissfully erotic.

Pulling me down to him, he sucks a nipple between his teeth and groans as I ride him hard. His hands clench my waist, and he moves me faster. Everything builds up inside me, and I hold back my scream as he too is milked to completion, his cock pulsating as he spills his warmth inside me.

Tate grabs my face and kisses me. "Holy fuck, that felt good. I needed it."

"So did I."

A car rumbles in the distance, signaling our time is up. Tate holds me in his arms for another minute before sliding off the bed and throwing on his clothes. "I love you, Faith."

He grabs the stone and his appearance shifts to Micah. "I love you too," I whisper. He hurries out the door, and I close my eyes. We have a plan, but we don't know if it'll work yet. Our fate will be decided tomorrow.

THIRTY-THREE

TATE

Looking in the mirror is strange, especially when I see Micah's face staring back at me. If I had to pretend to be Micah for the rest of my life, I'd do it just to have time with Faith. It killed me knowing she was just next door to my room, and I couldn't be in there with her. At least, I knew she was safe. I haven't left her side the entire day.

"When do you think we'll find out?" Faith asks as we sit down at the dining room table filled with all sorts of food. It's closing in on seven o'clock, and no one has heard who is fighting who.

Colin grabs a plate and piles it high. "Obviously, Vilkas likes to keep everyone on the edge of their seats."

Two seconds later, Killian strolls into the dining room with Tia. "I do, actually. It keeps things interesting."

Tia gives Faith a reassuring look and joins us at the table. I stand close to Faith as we fix our plates. With Micah being her protector, it gives me an easy excuse to stay by her side. Faith sits down and I next to her while Killian takes the chair across from us.

"The fight starts in an hour. It'll be against Dixon."

I can feel her relief through our bond. She nods and picks up a piece of asparagus. "Think you'll win?"

He bursts out laughing. "Of course, I do. I'm hoping you want me too as well."

"Are you still going to let me go?" she asks.

The genuine look on his face is fake as hell. He's not fooling anyone. "If that's what you wish."

She snaps off the edge of her asparagus with her teeth. "That's all I wanted to hear." Her disappointment is palpable. One of the things I love about her is her willingness to help others. She was ecstatic when Orin backed out of the fights. A part of me wonders if she's hoping she can help Killian with his rage, but even I know he's too far gone. There's an emptiness in his eyes from the darkness. I've seen what the rage does to unmated males. It eats away at you until there's nothing left.

Roman walks into the dining room and pockets his phone. "Just told Grayson he's fighting his second-in-command tomorrow."

Killian chuckles and gets to his feet. "That'll be one hell of a fight. I wish I could sell tickets."

"How did you get him to turn against Grayson anyway?" I ask. It's strange hearing my voice sound like Micah's.

He smiles over at Roman and then laughs again when he turns to me. "Money and power. How else? You wouldn't believe all the people I've seen turn on those they love because of it. I was just about to give up searching for Faith when I end up at the same bar as Anson. He was babbling on and on about how his alpha wouldn't share a certain royal he had in his grasp. I knew then it was fate." He turns his gaze to Faith. "I approached him with my plan, and he was all too willing to disclose where you were. It was his idea to do the video at his house."

So that's how it happened. "Does Anson think he's going to beat Grayson?"

Killian snorts. "Their technique is similar, but Tate's a much better fighter than him."

"What about you? Do you think you're a better fighter?"

He shrugs, but I can see the evil glint in his eyes. "Don't know. Guess we'll find out." He smiles over at Faith. "You could always use your influence with Tate. He's your friend, so I know he'll listen to you. You can tell him I'm going to set you free. There's no need for him to die senselessly."

Faith narrows her gaze at him. "You'd let him leave unharmed?"

"Of course. He can be put on a plane tomorrow night if you want."

"He wants me far away from you," I say to Faith.

Faith keeps her eyes on him but answers me back. *"I see that. It won't surprise me if he tries to send Colin and Micah away. Not unless he plans to incapacitate them while he has his way with me."*

Faith takes a sip of her wine. "I'll see what I can do. If he wins the fight tomorrow night, I'll talk to him."

Killian's grin widens. "Perfect. I should probably start getting ready for the fight. I'll see you down there in a few minutes."

As soon as he's gone, Faith glances over at me, but there are still wolves around within earshot. We have to be careful what we say. "Do you think Tate will give up?" she asks me, knowing damn well what I'm going to say.

"No," I answer. "He doesn't give up on anything."

Tia grabs a grape off of the fruit tray. "I just want to get through tonight. I've seen enough blood to last ten lifetimes." We all finish our food, and Faith latches onto my arm as we walk outside to the underground pit. Tomorrow is my day, the day I have to kill a man who's been like a brother to me my entire life.

It has to be done.

THIRTY-FOUR

TATE

The day went by quicker than any day I've ever experienced before. One minute, I'd look at the clock, and the next, an hour had passed. Faith stayed by my side all day, trying her best to get my mind off of what I'm about to do.

With her on my arm, we walk into the underground pit. Everyone sees me as Micah. As soon as he arrives, we'll have to switch places. "Anson's already here," Faith says.

I follow her line of sight, and he's surrounded by several of Killian's wolves, laughing and carrying on as if he's not getting ready to die. "I see that," I growl low. I walk her over to her seat, and Tia sits down next to her.

Tia looks up at me. "You know the plan, right?"

I nod. "Got it."

Once Micah shows up, looking like me, I'm to go to one of the back rooms so I can hide my stone and turn into myself. She'll retrieve it and give it to me after the fight so I can go back with Faith. All I have to do is do one of the hardest things I've ever had to do in my life. Colin walks into the pit and heads straight for us.

"Tate just got here," he says to me.

I look down at Faith, and she smiles sadly. *"I'll see you afterward."*

Colin goes with me to the back room, which has a couple of showers as you'd see in a gym. He hands me a pair of shorts he had hidden under his shirt. Since we can't say anything with all the shifters close by, he nods, and I nod back. A few seconds later, Micah marches in, and I toss him my stone so he can hide them where Tia told us to. Looking in the mirror, I'm back to myself. Micah changes into the clothes I was wearing, and I put on the shorts.

"Will you show him mercy?" Colin asks.

Visions of him in the library with Faith run through my mind. "No. He doesn't deserve it."

Micah places a hand on my shoulder. "I wish it didn't have to be this way. We'll see you after the fight."

Roman slams a hand against the door. "Times up, Grayson. Let's go." Colin and Micah both leave, and I take a deep breath. It's time to end this.

I walk out, my sole focus on the task at hand. Gasps and cheers erupt when I enter the pit, but I block them out. Faith's mind is quiet, and I know it's because she doesn't want to distract me. Anson climbs up into the ring, and our eyes lock. He doesn't even look like the same man I've known my entire life. The leer on his face and the outright deceit makes me hate him with every fiber of my being. He betrayed me.

I march up the stairs onto what used to be a white mat. Now it's stained with shades of red. In the past few days, so many shifters have lost their lives where I stand.

Roman grins and holds out his arms. "It's all yours, gentlemen. Anything goes." He steps out of the ring and locks the cage door.

The crowd's cheers rumble all around us, their feet

stomping on the concrete floor to spur us on. I'll fight when I'm damn well ready. "Is this how you pictured it?" I snap.

Anson circles the ring, and I counter his movements, making sure to stay one step ahead of him. "I want what I want, brother." His eyes shift over to Faith. "It's time I finally get it."

My body trembles with the need to turn, but I lunge and punch him right on the side of the face. His head snaps to the side, and I grab his neck. "I'm not your brother."

THIRTY-FIVE

FAITH

Tate attacked first, and he didn't stop with just one punch. I thought they would shift into their wolves, but they didn't. This is personal. Anson is strong, and he matches Tate with every single blow. They look like a blur in the ring, the sound of fists pounding flesh. I thought watching wolves tear each other apart was worse, but I was wrong. It breaks my heart to see two men who were like brothers battle it out to the death.

"This is going to be a long fight," Micah whispers. "Tate's going to want to punish him."

Swallowing hard, I nod. "I know."

The smell of blood permeates the air, both Anson's and Tate's. Anson kicks Tate in the shin, and he goes down for only a split second. Anson uses that advantage and slices his claws across Tate's back, blood pouring like rivers down his skin.

Tia squeezes my hand and averts her gaze away from the ring. "I thought I could stomach this. It's worse than all the others."

I have no doubt Tate will win, but it's the emotional aspect of the fight that's mentally draining. In Tate's mind, he knows what he has to do, but his heart isn't in it. The wound from a betrayal that deep will leave a scar that nothing can heal.

The world moves in slow motion as I watch Tate and Anson fight to the death. Tate's claws slice through Anson's stomach, but both keep fighting as if they aren't bleeding out all over the mat. Tate never flinches in pain; he just keeps striking as if nothing's amiss. My breaths are all I can hear. I look around at Killian and his men all cheering like animals. What kind of world revels in this kind of madness? There's only one word to describe it ... hell.

In Tate's mind, I can feel his need for revenge. Both men fall to the mat, grappling around in their blood. It goes on for what feels like an eternity, and all I want is for it to be over. Tate gets the advantage and climbs on top of Anson with his arms around his neck.

"I hope it was worth it," Tate growls. "You lost."

Anson's face turns red, and his eyes blaze. His body shimmers on the verge of shifting, but Tate digs his claws into Anson's neck just like I did. However, this time, Tate rips him apart. Thunderous roars echo all around us, but Tate doesn't revel in it; he just killed his best friend.

Closing my eyes, I push into his mind. *You did what you had to do.*

Covered in blood, Tate slowly stands, and his claws retract back into his hands. He looks over at me with pain-filled eyes. *I'm starting to think I never knew him.*

Roman unlocks the cage, and two of Killian's men climb inside to take away Anson's mangled body. Tate watches them, his face emotionless as he steps out of the ring and looks down at the blood covering his skin. Roman joins him and motions for him to go to the back. Tate glances over at me before disappearing around the corner.

I'm going to get cleaned up. Send Micah and Colin back.

Okay, I murmur.

I nudge Micah in the side, and he already knows what to do. He and Colin disappear to the back, and I stay with Tia. "Is he okay?" she asks.

"He will be."

Killian comes over with a big wolfish grin on his face. "That was a fascinating fight. Very entertaining."

It gets harder and harder to pretend to be amenable around him. Especially knowing he plans to hinder me and mate with me on the full moon. I guess he thinks I'd wake up the next morning and accept him as my mate. The problem is that I wouldn't be able to kill him if Tia's still linked to him. I'd be a prisoner for the rest of my life.

"I wouldn't call it entertaining," I grumble. "It was a tragedy."

Killian shrugs, not caring in the least. "Are you going to talk to Grayson about going home?"

I nod. "I am, but I don't think he'll believe me if I tell him you have honorable intentions about letting me go."

His smile fades. "That's a shame. I'd hate for you to lose a friend."

A few minutes later, Tate, Micah, and Colin appear from the back and walk toward us. Micah smiles at me, and I already know it's really Tate. I open my arms for Tate, and Micah hugs me. "You owe me big time for this."

"I know," I whisper. I stand back and plaster on a smile. "You fought well."

Killian comes over and pats him on the back. "Good job, Grayson. I'm impressed."

It's interesting seeing Micah as Tate. "Thanks," he says, his voice sounding bored.

Killian points over at me. "Faith has something she'd like to talk to you about. I'll give you some time alone."

Once he's gone, Micah stares at me through Tate's eyes and pretends to be curious. Both he and Tate already know what Killian wants. He wants Tate to go home. With Killian close by, I know he can hear us. I go through the spiel, and the outcome is exactly as I thought it would be. Tate's going to stay.

I glance back at Killian and shake my head. Killian comes over and shakes who he thinks is Tate's hand. "Guess I'll see you tomorrow night."

Micah smirks. "Yes, you will."

Killian snaps a finger, and Roman comes over with Barrett. "My men will take you back now."

Micah turns to me, and I hug him again. "I'll see you soon." He is right. I'm going to owe him big time after all of this is over. The problem is that nothing can measure up to everything he's done for me. We watch him leave with Roman and Barrett, and it makes me nervous to see him go. I have this fear that I'll never see him again.

"You will," Tate says. He stands close to me, and everyone assumes he's Micah as we walk out. *"This will all be over tomorrow."*

It all seems like the perfect plan. We'll complete the bond at sunset, and he'll defeat Killian because the link to Tia will break. Unfortunately, there's a dreadful feeling in my gut that says it won't be so easy.

THIRTY-SIX

FAITH

The night came and went, and I wasn't able to sleep a wink. That feeling in my gut grows stronger by the minute. While Tate worked out with Colin to get ready for the fight, I walked around the gardens for hours, hoping nature would help me. Sunset will arrive within the hour, and Killian's house is crawling with wolves. If we can't complete our bond during the full moon magic, then we'll lose.

"I'm surprised there aren't wear marks on the pavers from where you've walked on them all day," Tia calls out.

Forcing a smile, I glance back at her. "Walking helps me think."

Tia's flowing navy blue dress blows in the wind, giving her an ethereal look. It's not only mine and Tate's lives in the balance, but hers as well. She takes in a deep breath and peers out at the mountains in the distance. "Yeah, it does help. The earth is a power source for me."

"You've never mentioned much about your family. Where are your parents?" I ask.

She nods toward the path, and we walk. I can feel her sadness. "I don't know. After they had me, I got to stay with them for eight years before Killian's family came. We lived in Quebec."

Her lips tremble, and I take her hand. "I'm sorry, Tia. You must really miss them."

"I do. They had no choice but to give me up. I can still hear my mother's screams when they took me away."

"Do you know if they're still alive?"

A sad smile spreads across her face. "I hope so. If our plan works and I'm set free, I want to find them."

I squeeze her hand. "You'll find them."

She looks up at the sky and grins. "Can you feel the moon?"

Its magic grows stronger by the minute. "I do."

"Let's go inside. The second the opportunity arises, I need for you and Tate to do your thing."

"So romantic," I laugh even though there's no humor to it.

Tia cups her other hand over mine. "There will be plenty of time for that."

"I hope so."

We walk into the house, and we both freeze when I hear Tate's name. Tia pulls me closer to the dining room where Orin and Killian are talking. "I have us shielded," she whispers so low I can barely hear her.

"Why do you look like that, Orin?" Killian huffs.

Orin sighs. "There's no reason to do this. You have Tia's magic."

"I'm ready for it to be over now," Killian growls. "I'm going to tell Faith that Grayson decided to go home. We'll go in, kill him, and be done with it. That way, everything can go as planned tonight when I mate with Faith."

My body boils with anger, but Tia clenches my hand tight. I'm not going to do anything stupid.

"I thought you were going to let Faith go? What happened to that?"

Killian chuckles. "Oh, Orin, you're so honorable. You know I was never going to agree to that. She's mine and always will be. When we're mated, I'll be one of the strongest shifters in the world; a royal."

"Faith will hate you for this." I would do more than hate him. I'd kill him the first chance I got.

Killian scoffs. "She'll learn to love me. I'm sure Tia has some kind of spell to help that along."

Bile rises up the back of my throat, burning like fire. Tia backs away from the door and pulls me up the stairs to my room. As soon as we get into my room, I concentrate on Tate. *"I need you and Colin, now."*

"On our way. I listened in."

A few seconds pass, and he comes storming in looking like Micah with Colin behind him. "We need to call Micah."

Footsteps pound on the stairs, and I know it's Killian by the raw power exuding from him. He knocks on the door and opens it, smiling when he sees everyone with me. "Ah, you're all here. There's food in the dining room."

Tia fluffs my hair. "I was just about to help Faith get ready for the big night. We'll be down in a minute."

Killian shakes his head. "No rush. I have to run into town for a little while. We have a little bit of time before the fight."

Tia's brows furrow. "Why do you have to go into town?"

His sly grin makes me sick to my stomach. "I just need to visit with someone. I won't be gone too long." He turns to me and rakes his gaze over my body. "You look lovely today, Faith."

"Thanks," I reply, trying my best to smile. He shuts the door, and I clutch my stomach. Until he's out of range of hearing us, we can't call Micah. I rush to the window and watch him leave with three of his other wolves. Orin stands there in the driveway until the gate closes, and then he heads back inside.

"Orin's still downstairs," I hiss. "He'll hear us." And just like that, his footsteps pound up the stairs, and he bangs on my door.

"Faith, we need to talk."

Tia opens the door, and he rushes in, glancing at everyone quickly. "There isn't much time. Call Grayson and tell him he's in danger. He needs to get out and fast."

Colin already has his phone out. I can hear Micah on the other end, but his voice sounds like Tate's. "They coming to pick me up already?"

"No," Colin snaps. "You have to get out of there. They're coming to kill you."

"What? What the hell happened? Do they want Tate or me?" Orin's eyes widen in confusion, and he looks at me, but I turn away. I don't know if we can trust him, but it seems like we might not have a choice.

Colin huffs. "No time to explain. Just get out."

"Fuck," Micah growls. "They're here. I'm going out the window."

"Where will you go?" Colin asks.

"To Faith. I'm her protector. I don't know how I'll get through the gate, but I'll find a way." The phone disconnects, and the room falls silent.

Orin clears his throat and stands in front of Tate, who looks like Micah. "If you are Micah, Faith's protector, who was that on the phone? It sounded like Grayson, but he didn't talk like him."

I step between them. "First off, why did you come here to warn us?"

Orin's eyes are full of regret. "You told me that if I start doing the right things, I'll find my redemption. I'm ready for it now. I disagree with Killian and what he's doing; it's wrong. Tate doesn't deserve to die like this. If he wants to fight for you, that's his choice. He should at least be able to make the decision for himself."

Colin steps up behind him. "If you so much as think about betraying us, I'll snap your neck without hesitation."

Orin's gaze doesn't leave mine. "You can trust me, Faith. I'm not only doing this for you, but for Tia as well."

Tia flings her arms around his neck. "You always were my favorite."

A genuine smile spreads across his face as he hugs her. "Tell me how to set you free, and I'll do it."

She lets him go. "Only Faith and Tate can do that." She holds out her hand to Tate. "Let me have the stone."

Tate looks down at me, and I nod. He hands Tia the stone, and his true form is revealed. Orin shakes his head and laughs. "I should've known Tia had a part in this."

I reach for Tate's hand and look over at Orin. "He's my mate, Orin. That's why we left for Florida. I knew he'd be a target until we could complete the bond."

Orin snorts. "Yeah, he would be dead in Florida right now if Vilkas knew."

Tia rushes over to the window, and I know it's only minutes before sunset. "It's almost time."

"Time for what?" Orin asks.

Tia pushes him toward the door. "If Tate's going to defeat Killian, they have to complete the bond. Guess it's a good thing he decided to leave the house."

They all stop at the door, and Orin focuses on Tate. "After you do this, what are we going to do?"

Tate stares down at me and then back to him. "I'm going to fight. I have to finish this once and for all."

Orin nods, and then his phone rings. He holds it up to show us it's Killian. "Yeah," he answers, putting it on speakerphone.

"The bastard escaped. Stay at the house in case he comes there. Either way, he's dead."

Orin sighs. "Will do. I'll make sure he doesn't get to Faith." He hangs up and slides the phone into his pocket. "Do what you got to do. I don't know how much time you have."

He walks out with Colin, and Tia grabs the door handle. "See you soon."

The door closes, and I look up at Tate. "When we're free of this place, I want to spend an entire day making love, okay?"

Tate smirks and cups the back of my neck. "I'm up for that." The full moon has a way of heightening everything. Scents are stronger, food tastes better, and when someone touches you, it feels incredible.

Placing my hands on his face, I kiss him hard, moaning in his mouth as he grips me tight. "I love you, Tate."

Growling low, he lifts me in his arms, never once taking his lips from mine. "I love you too." He tosses me onto the bed and covers me with his body. I love the feel of his weight pressing me into the bed. All I can smell is him all around me. I don't want the night to end, but we don't have time.

Tate sucks my bottom lip between his teeth and tugs on my shirt. "Let's get this off of you. I know we don't have long." He lifts my shirt and bra over my head, and I unbutton my jeans so he can slide them down my legs. My entire body aches for him. I watch him as he takes off his clothes and everything inside of me tightens.

He crawls up my body, and I nip his neck, rolling my hips beneath him, earning another deep growl to escape his lips. His fingers trace over my nipples, and my whole body throbs in anticipation. "I can feel the magic of the moon, pulling us closer together."

I look into his glowing blue eyes that darken with need. "I can too," I say, trembling with desire.

My need hits him hard, and it spurs him on. All I can hear

is my erratic breathing and the sound of his breaths as he touches me. It feels like his hands are all over my body, exploring me. It feels so good, I want to scream.

Bending down, he flicks a nipple with his tongue before closing his lips around it, sucking it greedily. Desire shoots through my veins, the heat of it coursing through my body. Tate rubs the tip of his cock between my legs, smiling when he feels how wet I am.

"How bad do you want me inside of you?" he asks, still licking my taut nipples.

"Probably just as bad as you want to be inside of me," I counter teasingly.

His lips pull back in a smile. "You have no fucking idea." He pushes the tip in just a bit, only enough to drive me wild. "I promise to make this last longer the next time."

Moaning, I lift my head and arch my back. "I don't care. Just make love to me."

Tate's deep-throated chuckle echoes throughout the room at the same moment he pins me to the bed with his weight. Grasping my face in his hands, he leans down and bites my bottom lip. "Happy to."

Plunging deep and hard, Tate moves his hips against mine, grunting with the sheer force of his thrusts. I counter his movements, rocking my hips just as hard. His arms cage me into his body, and he towers over me like I'm nothing but a small animal. I want more; I had to have more.

Wrapping my legs around his waist, I tilt my hips higher so I can get more of him in me.

"Harder, Tate," I cry.

He pulls back, concern mixed with raw passion in those glowing blue eyes of his. "Are you sure? I don't want to hurt you."

I bite my lip and nod. "I need to feel all of you." Lifting my knees, he tilts my hips up and pushes himself inside of me until we're fully connected. I can feel him stretching me, the magic engulfing us. "Is this what you wanted?" he growls low.

"Yes," I moan.

Faster and faster, he pounds into me, the orgasm building in between my legs. Raking my nails down his back, I hold back my scream as the final burst of pleasure spreads throughout my body. Tate pumps a couple more times, and I can feel him shudder and release his warmth deep inside, filling me up.

Breathing hard, he collapses on top of me and kisses me tenderly on the lips. I smile up at him, loving the fact that he's still hard between my legs. He reaches for my hands, and that's when I see the magical threads binding us together. It's like strands of glitter wrapping all around our bodies. Our souls connect as one. I thought I was strong before, but with his strength added to mine, I feel invincible.

"How do you feel?" I murmur.

He smiles down at me. "Like I can do anything."

Time is of the essence, and I know we have to be ready. "Let's finish this so we can go home. I'm ready to start living our lives together."

His hand brushes down my cheek. "I do too. You're my mate, and no one's going to take you away from me."

I shake my head. "Never."

WE DRESSED QUICKLY, and I could feel Colin and Orin downstairs. There are other wolves around the house, walking the perimeter. I'm pretty sure they know about Tate's supposed disappearance. Tate grabs his blue stone off the dresser, and he turns into Micah. He looks at himself in the mirror.

"I thought Tia's magic wouldn't work on us once we bonded," he says.

I shrug. "This magic helps us. You're choosing to use it. I think it's only with spells that are meant to harm that don't work."

"How shocked do you think Vilkas will be when I drop the stone?"

I snort. "Probably pretty damn surprised."

When we get downstairs, Orin and Tia stare at us curiously. "You look the same," Tia says to me, but then she smiles. "But you definitely aren't. I just tried to put you to sleep, and it didn't work."

She hugs me tight, and I smile. "We're ready."

Orin's phone rings, and he answers. "Did you find him?"

I can hear Killian on the other end. "Fuck, no. We're almost back at the house. Have Tia get Faith ready in the bedroom."

Tate tenses beside me, and I take his hand. Orin hangs up and sighs. "Well, you heard it."

Tate looks down at me. "Let's end this."

All of us walk outside. Tate stands next to me, still appearing as Micah. Orin and Tia flank us to the left and Colin to our right. "Are you sure you want to do this?" I say, looking over at Orin.

He nods. "You'll need backup. We all need to be prepared to fight. I don't know what the others will do when they see what's really going on."

Two cars approach the gate, and it opens. "What the hell's going on? Why are you all out here?" one of Killian's wolves says as he comes around the side of the house. I've never spoken to him, but his name is Brit.

Another wolf joins him, and Orin stands between them and us. "Stand down, boys. Not unless you want your balls shoved down your throats."

Brit's mouth gapes, and he stands back, clearly confused. The cars move closer, and I can feel Killian's angered energy vibrating from the vehicle. Tia's heart races, and I look over at her. "It'll be okay."

She blows out a shaky breath. "I'm not free yet. He can still command me."

The door opens and he storms out, eyes blazing as he glares at Tia. Roman and Barrett stand behind him, both on edge. I have a feeling it's not going to be just Killian and Tate battling it out. My wolf is desperate to break free.

"It seems like we have a miscommunication here," he announces.

I shake my head. "Not exactly. I didn't feel like waiting for you in your bedroom."

He turns his sneer to Orin. "Traitor."

Orin stands his ground. "You lost your way, friend. You can make it right by letting her go."

Killian rips off his shirt, his face contorting in outright rage. "She's mine. No one and nothing's going to stop that from happening."

Tate holds up the blue stone, drawing Killian's attention. He tosses it to the ground, and everyone's eyes widen when they see who he really is. "I'm going to stop you. You're not the only one who can use magic."

Fuming, Killian turns his anger to Tia. "You betrayed me. You'll regret it."

Orin stands protectively in front of her, and it infuriates Killian more. "Fine. We can finish this right here and right now. You can't beat me," he hisses at Tate.

Tate smirks and holds out his arms. "Oh, I think I can." His body shimmers and shifts to his true form. He used to be a solid gray wolf, but now he has my royal arctic blood flowing through his veins. Mixed in with the gray are strands of white, and he's much larger than he used to be.

Killian's growl echoes through the air. "How is that possible?"

"He's my mate," I shout. "My one true mate. You nor anyone else could stop it from happening."

His eyes glow a menacing green. "Unleash me, Tia."

Tia falls to the ground, screaming in pain. Orin wraps his arms around her and looks up at me. "She's trying to fight it."

"Unleash me!" Killian shouts, his feral power radiating all around me.

Tia has no choice but to give in. Killian bursts into his wolf, and Tia passes out in Orin's arms. Killian lunges for Tate, and it's all snapping jaws and claws. The second Roman and Barrett shift, I have no choice but to do the same. Tate may be stronger now, but there's only so much one can do with three wolves attacking you, one being feral.

Taking a deep breath, I give in to my wolf, loving the feel of her taking over my body. It's the first time I've shifted in weeks. She's strong and ready to fight for her mate. Roman roars and charges toward Tate, but I lunge through the air, tackling him to the ground. We roll around, and I take a bite out of his abdomen. He howls in pain and backs away from me. I tower over him, and he lowers his head, showing his submission. He only gets one chance. If he attacks again, I'll kill him.

Barrett and Killian attack Tate at all angles. His gray and white fur is matted with blood, but so are the other wolves.

"I'm going to take Barrett out."

Tate growls. *"Do it. I should've known they'd fight dirty."*

Barrett jumps onto Tate's back, and I sink my teeth into his leg, tossing him across the yard. He yelps in pain but growls when he looks at me. I growl back, showing off my fangs which are much larger than his. He rears back and runs for me, but I'm ready for him. I've been training to fight my entire life. Micah taught me well.

I'm about to deliver the final blow when, out of nowhere, a giant white wolf slams into Barrett and rips out his throat. Micah. He pads over to me, staring at me with those blue eyes of his. I should've known he'd find a way to get through the gate.

None of Killian's other wolves shift. They stand on the sidelines, watching as their crazed alpha circles around Tate. *"We can take him out,"* I say to Tate.

"No. He's mine."

Killian snaps at Tate, and his moves are sloppy and erratic. That's what the rage does. Every time he lunges and tries to attack, Tate slides away with ease. He growls at the other men in his pack, but none of them make a move to help. That seems to anger him more. He jumps at Tate, and they roll around on the ground, snapping and clawing at each other. The second Killian's neck is exposed, Tate delivers the deadly strike. Killian's blood flows from his lifeless body, and the light dies from his eyes.

Tia sucks in a breath and clutches her chest. I run over to her and shift so I can hold onto her. "Are you okay?"

Tia rubs the spot over her heart. "It's gone. I'm free." Tears stream down her face, and she hugs me. "I'm finally free." She lets me go and hugs Orin.

Micah stays in his wolf form, but Tate shifts and pulls me into his arms. "It's over. Let's get the hell out of here."

"Yes," I cry, holding him tight. "I'm way past ready."

THIRTY-SEVEN

FAITH

"**I**s that everything?" Micah asks as he packs the last of my clothes into my suitcase.

I look around the room, and everything is empty. "That's it."

He zips up my suitcase and sets it on the floor. It was only two hours ago we were outside, fighting what will hopefully be the last fight of our lives. "I could've taken Barrett," I say, crossing my arms over my chest.

Micah shakes his head and smiles. "I know, but I'm your protector. It's my job. Plus, you've never killed anyone before. I like that innocence about you."

My eyes burn. "You're not my protector anymore, Micah. You're free."

He nods. "I know."

Uncrossing my arms, I sigh and hug him. "Have you thought about where you want to go?"

He hugs me tight. "I thought I'd leave for a while. Nobody's heard from Raelynn or the others. I really want to find them, especially after all this happened with you."

"Who's Raelynn?" Tate asks, appearing at the door. Micah lets me go and glances back and forth at us. Sheepishly, I look away for a second, hating I kept that secret from Tate. Tate's eyebrows lift, and he leans against the doorframe. "Secret, huh? I heard that."

Micah clears his throat awkwardly. "All right, that's my cue to leave. I'll see you both downstairs." He grabs a couple of my suitcases and walks out.

"Raelynn's a royal," I confess. "And she's not the only one. I wanted to keep them safe."

Tate comes in and takes my hands. "It's okay. I don't blame you for keeping it from me."

"I hope they're okay. I don't like that Micah can't find them."

He pulls me into his arms. "If anyone can locate them, it'll be him." He kisses my forehead. "Is that your last bag by the door?"

I nod. "Yep. I'm ready to get the hell out of here. Is Chase's jet ready?"

Tate grins. "James is already at the airport. He asked me if I had a good vacation."

Laughing, I walk with him out the door. "And what did you say?"

"I said it was kind of boring. James believed it. I think he's more ready to leave Baker's Ridge than we are."

We get downstairs, and Colin holds up a duffle bag full of money. "What do we want to do with this?" With forty-eight fighters at two-hundred and fifty thousand each, it totals out to be twelve million dollars.

Tate looks at me and shrugs. "We'll do whatever you want."

"Let's give it to charities. We have plenty of money." Colin agrees with a nod and carries the bag out to the van. Tia's not in the foyer, so I head to her room while the guys finish loading our things in the car. Her door is shut, so I knock lightly. "Tia?"

"You can come in. I'm just looking around."

I open the door. "Do you have anything else that needs to be loaded?"

She glances at me over her shoulder and shakes her head. "No. I gave Colin the last of it." Blowing out a sigh, she peers around her room. "This has been my home for so many years. It feels strange leaving it."

"You'll like Montana. I promise."

She smiles. "I know I will. I'm not going to know what to do with my freedom. I can come and go as I please. Colin even said he'd take me out on a motorcycle."

Laughing, I shake my head. "Of course, he did. That's my brother for you. We'll be experiencing a lot of new things together. There's a lot I haven't done."

"I look forward to it." She takes one last look around her room. "All right, I'm ready."

All the guys are waiting by the front door when we arrive, except for Orin. "Has anyone seen Orin?"

Tate reaches for my hand. "No."

I can't help but feel a little disappointed. It would've been nice to tell Orin goodbye. "Guess we should go then," I say.

We all head outside, and Tia climbs into the back with Micah while Colin gets in the driver's seat. I'm about to get in when Orin's voice catches my attention.

"Wait," he shouts. I jerk around, and he races toward us with a bag slung over his shoulders. "Do you have room for one more?"

Tia jumps out of the van. "You're coming with us?"

Orin turns to Tate and me. "I don't belong here anymore. If you don't mind, I'd love to find a home with your pack."

Happiness overwhelms me, and I fling my arms around his

neck. "That would be amazing." I let him go, and Tia hugs him next.

He winks at me. "Besides, someone has a promise to live up to. You know, the one where you said you'd help me find a mate?"

"I haven't forgotten," I reply, grinning. "I don't break my promises." Tia takes his hand and pulls him into the van. Once we're all in, Colin drives us away. I don't even look back at the house when we exit the gate. "What will become of the Blue River pack?" I ask Orin.

He sighs. "Not sure. No one's alpha enough to take over other than myself, but I don't want the job. Who knows, maybe they should go their separate ways."

Maybe. Maybe not. It's not my responsibility to clean up Killian's mess. Still, I worry about all shifters. I'm a firm believer in second chances. Orin's getting his, and I know he deserves it. I just wish I could've helped others to get theirs as well.

Tate drapes an arm over my shoulders, and I breathe a sigh of relief. We're finally on our way home. The nightmare is over.

THIRTY-EIGHT

FAITH
ONE MONTH LATER

So much has happened since being back in the states. Tate spent a week with my family so I could say my goodbyes and make the transition to the Great Plains Pack. Even Tia joined us and had a wonderful time practicing magic with Laila. She and Kami have become good friends, and they live together now. I think Kami being in medical school is rubbing off on Tia. She's even thinking of going to college. Orin, on the other hand, has found a place with Grayson Construction. He fits in well with the others in the pack, and I can honestly say he looks happy.

Micah is still on the road, searching high and low for the missing royals. Every day I keep thinking I'll hear from him with good news, but it's always the same. Nothing. I keep thinking of Killian and how there are probably other shifters out there crazy enough to do the same things he did.

"You coming in, love?" Tate shouts.

I squint my eyes against the sun and watch him swim around in the crystal blue water. It's our first vacation as a mated couple. We've decided to take short trips every month so we can see the world. Right now, we're in the Turks and Caicos. Next month, we're going to Iceland.

Brushing off the sand on my thighs, I get up and join him in the ocean. He pulls me into his arms, and I wrap my legs around his waist. "When we get home, you have a lot of painting work lined up. I think I had three calls last week asking if you'd do custom paint jobs in their nurseries like you did at Jason and Anna's. Hope you're ready for it."

I kiss him. "Oh, I'm ready. I love painting nurseries."

His hands slide down to the backs of my thighs, holding me tight against him. "Speaking of babies, what are your thoughts on having some of our own? It could happen any day now."

I laugh. "Of course, it could. We've been putting forth quite the effort." Cupping his face in my hands, I look right into his bright blue eyes. "Whenever it happens, we'll be ready. You'll make a great father."

"And you'll make an amazing mother," he says in my mind.

He bounces me against him, and I smile when I feel how hard he is. "You seriously want to do that here? Like right now in the ocean?"

"Why not? Nobody's around," he says, chuckling.

I press my lips to his. "I have a strange feeling we're going to hear the pitter-patter of little feet soon if we keep this up."

He winks. "Hey, I'm fine with that."

So am I.

THE END
More Royal Shifters will be coming soon!

ABOUT THE AUTHOR

New York Times and USA Today bestselling author L. P. Dover is a southern belle living in North Carolina with her husband and two beautiful girls. Everything's sweeter in the South has always been her mantra and she lives by it, whether it's with her writing or in her everyday life. Maybe that's why she's seriously addicted to chocolate.

Dover has written countless novels in several different genres, including a children's book with her daughter. Her favorite to write is romantic suspense, but she's also found a passion in romantic comedy. She loves to make people laugh which is why you'll never see her without a smile on her face.

You can find L.P. Dover at www.lpdover.com
Email: authorlpdover@gmail.com

ALSO BY L.P. DOVER

SECOND CHANCES SERIES

Love's Second Chance

Trusting You

What He Wants

(Trusting You Prequel)

Meant for Me

Fighting for Love

Intercepting Love

Catching Summer

Defending Hayden

Last Chance

Intended for Bristol

ARMED & DANGEROUS SERIES

No Limit

Roped In

High-Sided

CIRCLE OF JUSTICE SERIES

Trigger

Target

Aim

In the Crossfire

ARMED & DANGEROUS/CIRCLE OF JUSTICE CROSSOVER SERIES

Dangerous Game

Dangerous Betrayals

Book 3 - TBD

Book 4 – TBD

GLOVES OFF SERIES

A Fighter's Desire

Part One

A Fighter's Desire

Part Two

Tyler's Undoing

Ryley's Revenge

Winter Kiss: Ryley and Ash

Paxton's Promise

Camden's Redemption

Kyle's Return

SOCIETY X SERIES W/HEIDI MCLAUGHLIN

Dark Room

Viewing Room

Play Room

FOREVER FAE SERIES

Forever Fae

Betrayals of Spring

Summer of Frost

Reign of Ice

ROYAL SHIFTERS SERIES

Turn of the Moon

Resisting the Moon

Rise of the Moon

BREAKAWAY SERIES

Hard Stick

Blocked

Playmaker

Off the Ice

STANDALONE NOVELS

Easy Revenge

Love, Lies & Deception

Going for the Hole

Anonymous

Love, Again

Fairytale Confessions

THE DATING SERIES W/HEIDI MCLAUGHLIN

A Date for Midnight

A Date with an Admirer

A Date for Good Luck

A Date for the Hunt

A Date for the Derby

A Date to Play Fore

A Date with a Foodie

Printed in Great Britain
by Amazon